Forward

Christine Gill

Forward

edición personal

Primera edición,
diciembre 2010

Obra coordinada por
edición personal
C/ Vergara, 6, 1° A
28013 Madrid
Tels. 91 559 29 49 / 55 22
edicionpersonal@edicionpersonal.com
www.edicionpersonal.com
Diseño y maquetación: Hugo Sánchez Maqueta
Impresión: Publicep
ISBN: 978-84-9946-069-7
Depósito legal: M-52723-2010

Impreso en España

One long hot summer a few years ago Jane sat on the edge of a cliff, her eyes gazing across the sea; a deep orange colour glowed in the sky. The sun had just come up, it was a beautiful morning; the birds were singing a merry tune: she sat there for quite a long time, she wasn't quite sure what she was going to do, her thoughts were racing away in her head; then all of a sudden she knew what she was going to do. It was time she went home and put the plan into action. She got very excited when she realized that this could be one of the biggest changes in her entire life. She must have been there longer than she thought, ought, she looked at her watch and could not believe the time. "Goodness, that time already! I must go and get some lunch." It was a lovely walk back to the small hotel where she was staying; it was run by a Spanish couple, she told them of her plan over dinner and they said it sounded as though she had made up her mind.

"I think I have," she said. "Can I make a phone call to my husband, Ben, please?"

"Yes, of course you can, my dear. Take as long as you like."

"Oh, I won't be that long; only I can't wait to tell him. He said when I had made up my mind I was to phone him."

"In that case why don't you make it in our lounge, it will be quite in there." "That's very kind of you; I will pay for the call."

"I will show you where it is."

When Jane came back they were waiting for news. "Well, what did he say?" The look on her face told it all, they gave her a big hug! "There is some coffee in the drawing room and some biscuit's. What time is your flight tomorrow? We will take you to the airport."

"That's a thought. I must ring them to find out the times have not changed. All this excitement, I forgot all about it."

"When you get back we will send you some brochures; what part of Spain are you looking at?"

"We were thinking of southern Spain, actually."

"So if you are around this area you will be able to come and see us."

"Of course we will, you have been so kind to me and it will be good to have some contact over here, don't you think?"

"Yes, it would, Jane."

"Well, I had better ring the air line now. I will see you later, I shall be in for supper; it will be my last night for a while. Bye now."

Jane went out into the lovely sunshine that afternoon with her head in the clouds, she was a very happy person. The birds were still singing a merry tune and she felt like joining them, she couldn't wait to get home and start the ball rolling. When she

phoned the airline there was no change in the times. She walked back to the hotel and found Paul talking to a customer, later she found out that the lady was well known in the area. In the evening she found herself talking to her, she found out that she was one of the properties agents. Her name was June, a very nice lady, and she knew all the steps. Jane wanted to know every thing about buying a house in Spain and how long it would take. She made a note of Jane's particulars and told her that she would be in touch. Jane went to find Mary and told her the news.
"Oh, good;" she said. "I know that lady: she often comes in here for her afternoon tea!"
"Well, if you give me your telephone number I can let you know when we have sold our house. Mary is going to send me some brochures; we are going to put the house on the market for 155 thousand pounds. I think we should get a house over here for that, don't you?"
"Oh, I am sure you will. There are very good prices over here at the moment, and I will keep a look out for you. Don't worry; you will be over here before you can say Jack Robinson! Now I suggest you must go to bed, you have a long day tomorrow."
"Yes I think I will."
"Do you want a nightcap? To help you sleep?"
"Oh, that would be lovely. A brandy would go down a treat."
"What time is your flight?"
"I am to be there at 4 p.m. in the afternoon!"
"Right, I will drive you, no need for a taxi."
"You're most kind. I will say good night now; see you all in the morning."
"Poor love, she is so excited I don't think she will sleep tonight." But she was quite wrong, as soon as Jane had her brandy she was fast asleep. Dave came down to reception to take over, all was quiet, he did his rounds and went back to the quiet lounge. It was a good shift, he had only one phone call for a booking the following day. Jane was up bright and early looking out of her bedroom window, the sun was still shining, and she got dressed and went down for breakfast. She was starving and thirsty, she couldn't wait to get home to Ben. They were to put the house on the market as soon as they can, in a month from now they should be over again to look for properties. After breakfast Jane went upstairs to finish her packing, then she went for her morning walk, when she had every thing under control she would buy herself a dog, but she would have to get organized first. At about 1 o'clock she went back to the hotel for her lunch, soon she would be on her way to the airport. But before she left she had a visitor, Mary had come to see her to give her some information on properties in the area and prices, she thanked her and said they would be talking again soon.
"It looks as though things are moving all ready; all set for your flight home, Jane?"
"Yes, ready as I ever will be!"
"Right, then away we go by for now, Paul." They made good time getting to the airport and soon it was time to say goodbye, telling Mary that she would be phoning her soon. She made her way towards the check in desk; everything went smoothly, thank goodness. She made her way up to the departure lounge to await

her flight, she was feeling very lonely. Soon her flight was called, she had to go to gate 9 to board the plane, and once on board she found her seat number and sat down. She brought a good book to read, but as soon as she started reading she fell asleep: with all the excitement she was exhausted. Half way through the flight the steward woke her up for a drink and some sandwiches, which she enjoyed. There was a film show on the small screen and it wasn't long before she heard the captain say they were approaching Luton. The weather was sunny, it was still quite light, the plane came down with a thud and the wheels touched down, they had to wait for the plane to come to a complete stop, and the doors were open. Once open they were allowed to go down the steps. They made their way to wards the arrival to collect their luggage and have their passports checked. When they came out of the terminal, Ben was waiting for her. She ran to him and he put his arm around her, and he asked her if she had a good time and a good flight over, yes of course she did.

"They took care of me very well. I have lots to tell you but I am afraid it will have to wait till tomorrow; I am almost dead on my feet, at this rate you will have to carry me out."

They found the car and soon they were heading for home. It was good being back in good old England, but she knew she had made the right choice.

"A nightcap, Jane?" said Ben.

"No, thanks, love, I am away to bed. I am going to have a lie in in the morning."

"I will be up soon, love," Ben sat for a while, thinking about the move. He hoped he was doing the right thing, however time will tell. He put out his pipe and locked up, and then he went up to bed. Jane never moved when he went into the bedroom, she was dead to the world. She looked so happy. Ben kissed her forehead and he too went to sleep happy that his wife was by his side again. In the morning Jane woke wondering where she was.

"It's alright, love, you're home again now, remember? Nothing to worry about, there is a cup of tea on the side for you, love."

"You're spoiling me."

"Don't worry; things will get back to normal. I am just going to ease you in gently and don't forget we are going to the estate agent."

"Oh, don't worry. I have not thought of any thing else."

"We had better phone mum and dad and let them know of our plans. They knew we were thinking of going to Spain, they will need time to get used to the idea. They will be able to come over for short breaks during the year. Are you going to phone or shall I?"

"I will, Ben. I can not wait to hear her reaction." Jane went off to do the phoning while Ben got the car out. It was still very warm, June was always a good month, let's hope someone out there wants to buy a house. Jane came hurrying out to Ben.

"Well, how did they take it?" asked Ben.

"Mum didn't sound too surprised, Ben. They wish us luck at the estate agents, we were to let them know we get on."

"Are we ready to go?"

"Yes I am!" said Jane. They had to wait a while before someone could see them, they were offered a cup of coffee, they saw some brochures on the decks and they were surprised how much the properties had gone down in Spain.
"When I was over there, June did say they were coming down, now is the time to buy."
"Right sir, sorry for the delay, we can see you now."
"Thank you, we would like to put our house on the market today. We are hoping for a quick sale."
"How much are you putting it on for?"
"Oh, about 155 thousand pounds."
"Right, I will just take down some details about your house. Is it semi or detached?"
"Semi, with 4 bedrooms, bathroom, shower, lounge, and double glazed, garden back and front, also a greenhouse, oh, and double garage, gas central heating, wall insulation…"
"Goodness me, it sounds a very good property to sell at that price; it will soon go. Where are you moving to?"
"We are emigrating to Spain, as soon as the house is sold."
"Gosh, how exciting," she said. "I don't blame you; they have very good medical teams out there. Let's hope we get your house sold soon. We will get the board up this afternoon and get someone over to check your house and take some photographs. It will properly be tomorrow or Wednesday, we will give you a call when he is free. Will that be?"
"Alright by us," said Ben.
"Right, we will be talking to you soon. Bye for now."
Thank goodness that's done, all we have to do now is hope we get a viewer soon and then we can get the ball rolling. Keep our fingers crossed, and all goes well tomorrow. I think this deserves another lunch out, than we shall have to tighten our belts."
They went to one of their favourite restaurant.
"Hello," said the waiter. "You're looking pleased with yourselves. What have you been up to?"
"We have just put our house on the market, Bob."
"Well, I heard you were in Spain Jane but I never thought for a moment you were thinking of moving out there. Good luck to you both and let's hope you get the house sold soon. I will keep my ears open and let you know what comes up, you never know! Now about your meal, what would you like?"
"I think I will have pork, please"
"And I will have beef," said Ben.
"It won't be long. Well, I never fancy them going off to Spain, well, well!" He was still talking to himself as he went to order their meal.
"I think he is quite shocked about us moving," Jane said.
"Yes, it seems so, Jane."
While they waited for their meal they had a quick look at the brochures, there were some lovely houses and bungalow, and the prices were not too bad either.
"You know, Jane, I think it might be a good idea if we went over there next month and have another look at the area and some houses, I have a feeling that the house won't take that long to sell."

"Oh, do you really think so?"
"Yes, I do. Oh, look, here comes our meal. It looks very nice. Do you want some wine with your meal?"
"Yes, please. You know, in Spain you have wine with every meal; it's really cheap out there."
"That's good. We will be able to save some money then." They paid their bill and went to do some shopping, and then they made for home. When they arrived home they got a surprise waiting for them, they had been to put the board up. Now they were sure things were going to move fast. As soon as they got inside the phone rang and it was the estate agents telling them that they would be sending someone out tomorrow to do a survey on the house, about 2 p.m.
"There, what did I tell you?"
"Yes, I know. We have a long way to go; I am going into the lounge to do some reading. and have another look at the brochures."
"What are we looking for?"
"A nice bungalow with a small garden near the beach." Just a minute the phone's ringing again. That phone has never stopped since I have been home. I am on my way. Who's speaking? Oh it's you, mum, what is the matter? Are you alright?"
"Yes, I am alright, I just wanted to know how you got on at the estate agents this morning."
"Oh, alright, thanks. The board's gone up already and they think it will sell quickly."
"Well, it has been looked after very well, you have both done a lot of work on it this year. It always helps when a property has been looked after. First impression always counts, you know."
"Yes, mum, I do, but thanks for the advice. We will keep you informed, don't worry."
"Oh, but we do. We only want to see you settled and happy."
Late in the afternoon they had another call from Mary. She said that she had a property that might be just up their street; it was on the market for 125 thousand euros.
"Did you here that?" said Jane, excited.
"What was that, dear? Did you say something?"
"Mary was on the phone. She said that she has found a bungalow for us."
"How much for?"
"125 thousands."
"That's a good price."
"She said it's not available till the end of October."
"Well, let's see first when we sell the house, dear. We could go out for our anniversary, what do you think of that?"
"That would be lovely, Ben, something to look forward too."
Ben smiled to himself. He was not going to hear the last about Spain for a long time to come, so he might as well get used to it. As long as Jane's happy that's all that matters, she means the world to him and she knows it. As they had dinner early in the day, a one-off thing, they had sandwiches, and fruit cake for tea washed down by a nice cup of tea, they watched a bit of telly, no more talk of Spain, thank goodness, and all was quiet in the Jones household. There was a good film on, called *A bridge*

to far; it was a sad film. It wasn't his kind of film so he went off to bed with a good book. Later Jane took him up a nightcap, but he was already asleep. *Poor old dear, he has had a tiring day. This move cannot come quick enough*, thought Jane. She had a shower and went to bed too. Once she got warm she fell fast asleep. The alarm clock went of and Ben woke up with a start.

"Goodness, is that the time? I wanted to be up early to make a start on the garden, keep it tidy now the boards gone up." Jane brought him up some coffee and they sat talking for a while. "When we get over there, we shall have to find room for mum and dad. When the time comes they can live with us, can't they?"

"Of course they can, my love. I think though it will be quite a while yet: they are not that old, you know."

"I know, but we have to think of them too."

"We shall, dear. Now let's go down for breakfast, I am starving."

"Yes, so am I."

After breakfast, Ben went to get his morning paper. Even the newsagents knew about their move.

"Goodness me! It doesn't take long for news to get around, does it?" said Ben laughing.

"Well, when are you off to pastures new?" John asked Ben.

"As soon as the house is sold. We are going out in October to have a look at some property."

"Not wasting much time then, mate, are you?"

"What is the point in holding on? We're not getting any younger, you know.

"You can say that again," said John. "We wish you the best of luck and hope your house gets sold soon. I don't see that there should be any problem, I will let you know if I hear of any one wanting a house in this area, Ben."

"Thanks a lot, that would be a help. Must away now or Jane will think I have emigrated without her." John laughed.

"No fear of that, you two are joined at the hip, so to speak. Bye for now."

Once back home Jane greeted him with a smile: "They're doing a survey on the property tomorrow, the man is coming early than they said. They also might have a possible viewer coming round on Thursday, our first one."

"Don't get too excited. We will have loads more, I think, dear."

"I know, but it's very exciting. I can't wait till October."

"Well, I am sorry, dear, we must. There is a lot to do yet, you will see time will soon go. Now I am off to sort out the garden. I might go down to the garden centre and see what they have on offer."

"Alright, dear, but don't spend too much."

"I want it to look nice, properly we will stand a good chance in getting it sold. What are you going to do today?"

"Well, I am first doing the bedroom, then the bathroom. It's going to be hard work."

"Don't overdo it. That's all I am saying."

"See you later."

"What time dinner is?"

"About 1 p.m. Is that too early for you, love?"
"No, that will be fine, dear."
"Jill from the agency said Mrs. Rowen is coming around 3 p.m., she sounded very keen!"
"Oh, good, that sounds promising, getting the first one. Anyway, this isn't getting my gardening done. It's more urgent now."
"Bye for now, I will call you in for coffee."
Time went by so quickly Jane didn't hear the phone ring.
"Alright, I am on my way. Hello, who's speaking? Oh, it's you, Jean, did you have a lovely holiday in Greece?"
"Yes, thank you, we have just got back. What is this I have been hearing about? My big sister living in Spain, you must be very excited about it."
"Well, we were going to tell you when you came back from your holiday, but you beat me to it! I suppose you have been talking to mum. She is very excited for us, she thinks it's the right time, do you think it is?"
"Well, if it's what you and Ben want, then why not? It's you life and you are still young enough to enjoy it. I think it will be great for you were always the adventurous one."
"That's all I wanted to hear. I will tell Ben when he comes in from the garden, we have the board up already, Jane, and our first viewer is on Thursday."
"Goodness, you might be on the move by the end of the year!"
"It looks like it, love. I must go now, I have a hundred and one things to do and I have not started on the dinner yet. I'll phone you later in the week, bye for now."
Ben came in for his coffee which Jane forgot all about.
"Did you forget my coffee?" he said. "I am dry as a bone."
"My goodness, look as if you have been through a hedge backwards," laughing, Jane handed Ben his coffee.
"Oh, that's gone down a treat, any biscuit's in the tin? I am starving."
"Only have one, dinner won't be long."
"It's a lovely day out there, after lunch I think I will go up to the garden. What have you got for dinner, Jane?"
"I have just put the chops under the grill; it should not take to long. We will have to think of some easy meals to do now I am busy with the house."
"Who was that on the phone?"
"It was Jean, she has just come back from her holidays. She phone mum as soon as she got home; they are all pleased for us. I think they will be expecting a cheap holiday."
"I can't blame them, can you? I would expect the same. It will be fun showing them around."
"Yes, it would. Dinner will be ready in half an hour, love."
"Right, I will go and do some more work in the garden. 2 more hours should see me through."
Jane was busy putting the chips in the oven, and then got the vegetables out of the freezer. She had found a bottle of wine in the fridge which she forgot about. Soon it was all ready; she called Ben.

"This looks good, Jane. Oh, I see you have found the wine."
"Well, we have to get used to having it with our dinner, you know."
Ben laughed and said: "It looks as though you have picked up some Spanish habits while you were out there, what about the language?"
"That's not difficult, but they talk so fast."
"Yes, I know they do."
"The area where we might be living speaks English anyway, so it would not matter too much."
"I know; you're properly right, love. That dinner was nice. I am off now."
"See you later."
"Have a rest now, Jane; you're looking tired."
After the dinner pots were washed up, she took her tea into the lounge and put on the television, to her surprise she soon fell asleep. She didn't hear Ben come in.
"Hello, love," he said. "Have you had a nice sleep? I think all this excitement is wearing you out. Anyway, look what I brought you; I put it in the kitchen."
"Ben, you daft thing, it will help me no end with dinner problems. Thank you." She put her arms around him. "You are the best," she said.
"Look, there is also a cookery book with it too."
They had some more coffee in the lounge and sat down to watch television they like to watch *Countdown* in the afternoon. Ben told Jane all about John at the news agents.
"He was most surprised; he also said he would inform us if he hears anyone that might be looking for a house in this area."
"That's good of him," said Jane. "People are being very helpful. You don't realize how many friends you have."
"No, that's true, you don't. I think I will go and plant these flowers. Have you been out in the garden to see what I have been doing?"
"No, I haven't had time; I have been busy doing the bedrooms. You have enjoyed yourself, I have heard you whistling. I will be out in a second to have a look." Jane went to put the dinner pots away and then went to find Ben.
"There you are. It is looking lovely. I can't see any one not wanting to buy it, I think."
"I think so too."
At that moment the phone went again.
"You answer it this time Ben!!"
"I will be there a moment; I just want to finish this."
"Oh, that can wait. The phone, please, now."
"Yes, bossy boots," he said laughing. "I am on my way." He got to the phone. "Hello," he said. "Who is speaking, please?"
"It's the estate agent here again."
"Oh, hello, any problem?
"Nothing to worry about, Mr. Jones. It's just that another viewer wants to come round on Friday, will you be in?"
"I think so, what time does she want to come round?"
"Say about 3 p.m."

"That will be all right, we can go shopping in the morning. We will see you on Wednesday anyway."
He went back out in the garden where she was sitting on her new bench.
"You know it's a shame to leave this house now that everything is taking shape. Who was on the phone dear?"
"We have another viewer on Friday. They have lots of people making inquiries about our house."
"Right, I am going in now; it's turning cold. It will be tea time soon and it's getting dark early tonight." Although it was getting towards the end of September, the nights were getting colder. "I am having an early night said Jane."
"There is football on the telly, I think I might watch it," said Ben.
"See you later, Ben."
"Do you want a nightcap bringing up, love?"
"Not tonight, dear. I shall properly be asleep when you come up."
"All right, see you later then."
The football match was good he had some brandy and he too went to bed. Soon they were both asleep. They slept in later than usual. Ben was up first, and brought Jane a cup of tea.
"That's the third morning in a row you brought me tea in bed, tomorrow it's my turn."
"I shall hold you to that," said Ben smiling to himself. "Is that lady coming today?"
"Oh, gosh, she is, I almost forgot."
"Well, do not be long before you get up. I will do breakfast this morning, just this once mind."
"Thanks," said Jane. "You're a star."
"Well, I have been called some things, but never that." Ben went down to start breakfast.
"It smells good," said Jane. "I love the smell of bacon, you have done well."
"Right, what are we having for dinner? If I put it in the slow oven now it should be ready for 2 p.m."
"Have we got chicken, dear? And a few vegetables and roast potatoes. That will go down a treat, don't you think?"
"Yes, that should not take long."
Ben went out into the garden again to admire is work, talking about praising himself of his work he said: "Yes I think I have done a good job." He had not noticed Bob from the paper shop looking over the fence.
"Hello there, Ben. The garden's looking lovely. I can't see it not getting sold."
"Hello, Bob. I was so stuck in my gardening I did not see you there! Yes, you know we have a viewer this afternoon, as a matter of fact; we can't wait to see her reaction to it all. Jane's been working hard since she got back."
"Bless her, she's a good girl, and she thinks the world of you."
"Yes, I know she does, that's why I want to get this house sold, so I can spend more time with her. Oh, that sounds like dinner's ready. I brought her a slow cooker yesterday: she has been dying to try it out."

"Well, it smells good," said Bob. "It's making me hungry now."
Ben went in for his dinner: "It's soon come round to dinner time, Jane, it smells good too. How was that new cooker, love?"
"Oh, just the job, Ben: the meats so tender…"
"That's good; we will take it to Spain with us."
"We certainly will," said Jane. "Now let's get dinner dished up."
"What do you think of the house now?"
"It looks lovely; I have a feeling about this viewer. What time is she coming, Ben?"
"I told you earlier, 2 p.m., not long now, I will get washed up and then it will all be tidy. I can not do any more to it so she will have to take it as she finds it. Keep our fingers crossed. I will take our coffee in the lounge and read the paper. When I was out in the garden Bob popped his head over the fence, he said the garden was looking lovely. He brought the garden to life; he did not realize I had green fingers. He had a phone message from someone making inquires about our house; they are going to get in touch with the agent tomorrow."
"Well, I never," said Jane. "I never thought our house was so popular, but here we all ready having some interest in the house."
They finished their coffee, put the cups away. Suddenly the door bell rang.
"It must be them," said Jane with excitement. "You answer the door, Ben, I am too nervous."
"All right, he said, laughing. He answered the door, and shown them the way.
"Hello, Mr. Jones, this is Mrs. Rowen. Shall we go through to the lounge first?"
"Hello, this is Mrs. Rowen. How do you do?"
"Pleased to meet you. Feel free to look wherever you want to go. I have to go and make a phone call; my husband will answer any question you may want to ask. Would you like some coffee and biscuit's?"
"Yes, please we would thank you."
When Jane had finished making her phone call she brought in the coffee.
"Sorry I had to go off like that but it was an important phone call." Ben looked at his wife, like saying *it could have waited!* They continued to look over the house; they seemed pleased with what they saw. Well, Jane could not contain herself any longer; she had to ask what they thought of the house.
"It has all the right requirement that we are looking for. We have one more to look at tomorrow; we will certainly come back for a second viewing if that's all right."
"That sounds promising," said Ben. "Yes, it does. We have another viewer on Friday, we will try and get back to you before the weekend."
"Well, thank you for showing us around, Mr. Jones; we will be in touch soon."
Jane and Ben went into the lounge and talked non-stop about the afternoon development.
"It is very exciting, what happens if the second viewer wants to buy it?"
"Well, I suppose if they have the right money for it, it's theirs. We will have to wait and see, Jane."
"Now let's see what's on telly, shall we, love?"
"A good idea; we can't do any more till Friday anyway."

There was the usual stuff on the telly, one of them was football, so Jane went of to bed to finish her book; the story was getting to an exciting part. She could not concentrate on the telly. Ben came up later.
“Is that the book you were reading last night, love? You seem to be enjoying it.”
“Yes, I will finish it tomorrow night. We will have to contact June in Spain tomorrow, let her know that we might be over sooner than we thought.”
“Yes, we should have heard something by Saturday at least.”
“Oh, Ben, it’s all getting very exciting.”
“Yes, love. Now can we get some sleep? Night.”
“Night, dear.”
They woke quite late.
“Morning, dear,” said Ben. “Your turn for tea, I think.”
“All right, I am going.” She made the tea, and biscuit’s, her favourites. When she came back down the phone rang.
“On my way. Hello, Mrs. Jones here. Who’s speaking, please?”
“Mary here, from the estate agents. I have some good news: Mr. Rowan has made a firm offer for your house, at the asking price; we would like you to come to the office and sign some papers for us. Mr. Rowan has sold his; it will take around 6 weeks to finalize it all, then you are on your way.”
“That is really good news. I am so happy; I will go and tell my husband straight away. We will be in tomorrow sometime, Mary! Ben, Ben! Did you hear all that? We have done it, we have sold the house at the asking price!”
“Oh, love, that’s good news, don’t forget we have to phone June in Spain again now and see if the property we were looking at is still for sale, won’t we?”
“First I want to phone mum and dad, they will be thrilled to bits. All right, I will go now and make that phone call.”
Dad answered the phone, he was delighted for them: “I will tell mum when she comes in, love. I am so pleased for you both.”
Ben phone June in Spain and told her the news.
“Well done both of you. I had a gut feeling about your house, Ben. I will get back to you soon.”
They had breakfast, washed up the pots and had a second cup of coffee.
“Just going down to get the paper, Jane, won’t be long.” When Ben got to the paper shop he could not wait to tell Bob.
“Well done, mate! So you will be off soon then.”
“Yes, in about a month’s time, it depends on how quick the solicitors are, and the bungalow we were looking at is still for sale.”
“That is good news, don’t forget to come and see us before you go.”
“Of course we will, and you will have to come too and see us.”
“Don’t worry, we will be over like a shot.”
“Must go now, we are off to the estate agents this morning to sign some papers.”
“See you soon.”

* * *

"I am taking Jane out for dinner tonight. It is a surprise, she has worked so hard getting the house ready, now she can relax a bit, can't she?"
"When Jane married you, she married a good man."
"That's very kind of you to say so, dad. You know I will take care of her when we get to Spain."
"Yes, son, I know you will."
"Well, tell mum to phone us when she gets back, will you?"
"Yes, no problem."
In the afternoon they went down to the agents, to sign the first of the papers. All they had to wait for was Mr. Rowan to do his bit, once that was done then they were truly on their way. Late in the afternoon mum rang, she sounded very excited for them.
"Oh, love," she said. "Your very first viewer and it sold! I could hardly believe it, you clever things!"
"Yes, I still can't believe it myself. All that hard work had paid off."
"When are you going out, Jane?"
"Oh, it will be sometime in October. Why?"
"Well, I was thinking would I be able to come with you? I could do with a break myself. Would Ben mind, do you think?"
"Oh mum, that would be lovely; we have not spent a lot of time together this year. I will ask Ben and get back to you straight away. We will be driving over, so there will be plenty of room. What about dad, will he be able to manage on his own?"
"Well, it was dad's idea. Yes, I think he will be alright, it's only for a short while."
"Well, the sooner I get off the phone I can ask Ben, mum. OK!"
"Alright, dear," said mum laughing. "Bye for now."
When Jane went back into the room, Ben said: "Mum sounded very excited, love."
"Yes, she was. She was so pleased we have sold the house, and she asked me to ask you if we could take mum with us when we go in October."
"Of course we can. Why I did not think of that, I do not know. Ring her back and tell her it will be OK."
Jane rang mum straight back, she was overjoyed and she said she would start to get ready for the trip.
"But mum, it is not for ages yet."
"I know, dear, but one has to be prepared, you know."
"All right, you win; anyway we will see you on Sunday."
"OK, bye for now."
After Jane phoned mum, all they had to do then was waiting: that was going to be the hardest part. It was then in the being of August, 2 more months to wait, then they would be going house hunting. They did some shopping in town, and had coffee, then made their way home to dinner, as Jane had put some meat into the hot pot, when they open the door; the smell from the kitchen was mouth watering. Jane put the kettle on, and in no time at all they were sitting down to a wonderful meal.
"That was delicious," said Ben.
"I told you it would come in useful."

"You certainly did, Jane. Now I am going for a quite read of my paper."
"Oh, I'll make tea then, shall I?"
Ben laughed: "If you like, dear. Thank you."
Jane decided to wash up first, before she retired to the lounge. She brought the tea in later and found Ben fast asleep in his chair having a quite snooze with his news paper in his lap. She was not sure whether to wake him, but she need not to have worried; he woke up as soon as she came into the room. She put down the cups.
"Here we are, love. It's all this fresh air we have been getting lately. I am going to do some knitting."
"And I am going for a quick smoke on my pipe. I have to water my plants in the greenhouse; I have grown some tomatoes and carrots for mum. Oh, by the way, are we going for Sunday lunch with them this week?"
"Yes, we are, and I think Jean is coming over. I do not know about the children, they seem to go out with their own friends more these days."
"Well, I suppose they have out grown us oldies."
"Were not that old, you know."
"I was only stating a fate, dear. Anyway, I am off now. See you later, love. Have a nice rest now, you deserve it."
"Thank you, dear, you're most kind."
When Jane looked at the clock she could not believe the time, she must have fallen asleep too. Ben came in from the garden.
"It's getting cold out there, now I could do with a hot drink."
"I will put the kettle on and make some sandwiches and we will have some of that nice fruit cake I made earlier in the week."
"Oh, thank you, dear, that sounds a treat," and he went to put his arm around her.
"What was that for?" she said.
"Oh, I just felt like it," and she laughed.
A few minutes later she came through with the tea and cake. Ben was drawing the curtains.
"It's starting to get dark early now. It's getting towards the end of September."
"Yes, it won't be long before we are off to pastures new, you just can't wait, can you, love?"
"No, not now. I know mum's coming with us, it will be good showing her where we might be living."
"This cake is good," said Ben. "Is there any more left?"
"Yes, enough for tomorrow. I shall have to make some more."
"I shall look forward to it," said Ben.
"Do you want to watch your soaps? If you do there is a good football match on later."
"I think I will go upstairs and watch it."
"OK, love. Do you want a nightcap bringing up?"
"Yes, please, dear, that would be nice.
"See you later then."
The phone rang. Jane went to answer it: "Hello, oh, it's you, Jean! What is the matter?"

"Nothing is. I heard that you have sold the house, congratulations! When you get settled over there, could we come over and stay with you for two weeks?"
"Of course you can. After all, you are my sister: just because we will be living in a different country we are not going to disown you, every body can come over."
"I heard mum is coming with you in October."
"Yes, she is."
"It will do her good, Jane. We have been a bit worried about her lately."
"Yes, so have we. She is not getting any younger, neither of us are, age catches up on us before we know it."
Jean laughed and said: "You can say that again, will you be at mum's on Sunday?"
"I think so, what time will you be there?"
"About 2 p.m."
"OK, we will see you there and then we can have a girlie chat, bye for now then."
I think I will take up a nightcap and go up to bed, I wonder if Ben is awake, she said to herself. Ben was watching the match; he did not see Jane come in to the room, until she put the cups on the table. He looked up and said to her: "Goodness, you are up early. Anything wrong?"
"No, dear, just fancy an early night. I have to finish that book; it's getting to a very exciting part."
"You do not mind if I keep the match on, do you?"
"No I do not mind, love. Drink your nightcap, that will get you a good night's sleep."
In the morning Ben went down to make the breakfast, brought Jane up a cup of tea.
"Morning, dear," he said. "You had a better night, that night drink helped us both, I think."
"Morning, love. Gosh, I am thirsty."
"Well, here is your tea, get it down you while it's hot."
"Alright, dear. I will be down soon, what day is it?"
"Friday, why?"
"I keep getting the days mixed up this week."
"I am not surprised all that you have had to do, but now you can relax, surely?"
"I shall be glad when we get it all finalized, won't you, love?"
"Yes, but we have 2 more weeks yet, so just try and stay calm, dear, there, otherwise you will make yourself ill."
"Oh, do not worry, I shall not do that."
When Jane came down, Ben was already dressed; she looked at the clock, she could not believe it.
"Goodness, is that the time?"
"Yes, it is."
"Are we going shopping later?"
"Yes, we are. I want to go down to the travel agents, and pre-book our trip over; we have to book early."
"Now who is panicking?"
"I know I am."
"It will be one thing less to worry about."

"That is all I am thinking about."
"Right then I had better go and get myself sorted; I will be down in a minute."
"Do you want some more tea?"
"Yes, please."
Ben had washed up before Jane came down, which surprised her, as he did not often do that.
"Thank you for doing the pots, Ben, what are you after?"
"Nothing, dear, it will help us to get out quicker, that is all."
"Let me have this cup of tea, and then I am ready."
"I am just going to get the car out, love, won't be long."
He was back in two shakes, and soon they were off. It was a warm day with a south east wind; the car park was not full so they could park easily, as they went through the car park people stop them.
"We heard you were going to Spain, Ben. Have you sold your house yet?"
"Yes, we have, Jim. We are hoping to go in October, we have a house to look at over there, and we are taking mum with us."
"Oh, that will be nice for her. She has been looking a bit run down lately, it will do her good."
"Yes, we think so too, don't we, Jane? Well, it has been nice seeing you Jim; see you before we go perhaps."
"Alright," said Jim. "Bye for now." And they all went their separate ways.
"Some people are nosy, don't you think?"
"No, I don't think so. I think they are just jealous."
"Maybe they are" said Jane.
They went off in silence; they arrived at the travel agents and booked their passage. They were going from Portsmouth to Bilbao then on to Torrevieja.
"Now that's done are we going shopping?"
"Yes, dear, we are. Then we can go for a cup of tea."
"Good idea." It wasn't long before they we sitting down to a nice warm drink of tea.
"It makes a change from coffee" said Ben.
"Yes, it does," said Jane. "But you know in Spain they always drink wine or coffee."
"And how do you say that in Spanish?"
"Well, it goes like this: *café con leche, por favor*.
"Right," said Ben. "Got that, I think. We will have to go to a Spanish school and learn it properly, shan't we?"
"That way we will make some new friends, that will be a good idea," said Jane. "I think it's time to go home. I will phone mum tonight and let her know we have booked the ferry, she will be pleased."
Soon they were home; while Ben put away the shopping Jane went to phone mum.
"Hello, mum, Jane here. I am just phoning to let you know we have booked the ferry for October."
"Oh, good," she said, sounding very excited. "I can not wait, can you?"
"No, we can't. It will be fun showing you around the area and our new home. Well, I must go now, see you on Sunday.

"Love, bye for now."
Jane put the phone back on the hook.
"Well, what did mum say? Was she thrilled?"
"Oh, Ben, you should have heard her, she is so happy for us! She is the best mum in the world, you know."
"Yes, sweetheart, she is. Now come and sit down and have this coffee before it gets cold."
Just as Jane sat down the phone rang again.
"Now what?" said Ben. "There is never a quite moment lately."
"It could be important, I had better go and answer it" said Jane. She picked up the phone, it was the agent asking them if they can come and sign some more papers for them, when it will be convenient for them. "How about Friday?"
"That sounds fine. See you then, bye for now."
"I have made you some more coffee, now come and sit down."
"That was the agents; they want us to go in on Friday to sign some more papers. Is that all right love?"
"Yes, that's fine. We have done a lot of paper work lately."
"Wait till you get over there, there is loads to do. After it's all done we can come and go as we please, it will be fun sorting out the house and finding ourselves around."
On Sunday they went to see mum and dad, they made a big fuss of them.
"Come in, my dears, it's lovely to see you."
They could smell the dinner; mum had already put the kettle, as always, she was organized.
"Oh, someone else is at the door, be a love Jane and answer it."
"On my way, mum. Jean and Bill, come in, mum is expecting you."
"Oh, it's lovely to see you both; it is nice having all the family together at last."
"Hello, mum. How are you both and where is dad?"
"Oh, he is in the garden, he spends a lot of time there these days.
Jane and Jean looked at each other: "We will talk later."
"What was that, dear?"
"Oh, nothing, mum."
They all sat down to a lovely Sunday lunch.
"Who would like afters?"
"Oh, I think we have had enough, thank you, mum. Jean and I will wash up."
"Not before you have tea and tell us all your news about the house sale."
"It went quite quickly, didn't it? Which was good, we thought there was a slump in the housing market. I think the area had a lot to do with it; apparently there was a lot of interest in it, and the price was right too. We were very lucky."
"Right, Jane, shall we go and do the washing up?"
"Yes, all right. Be with you in a minute. Did you want to talk to me about something, Jean?"
"Yes, it's about mum actually. I don't think she is all that well. What do you think?"
"No, I don't think so either."

"I know she is glad for you to go to Spain but I think she will miss you, we all will, Jane, but you have to think of yourself. In any case, she can come out to you some times and dad too, if he wants to. Do you think she will tell you what's worrying her? She talks to you more than me, you know."
"That's true, she does. I shan't ask her today, she is enjoying herself and it might upset her. I will try and come back and talk to her another day."
"That's a good idea, Jane. I'll take the coffee back into the lounge."
Dad was sitting in his chair smoking his pipe, which he loved to do. Bill was talking to mum, they were discussing the forthcoming event.
"You know, dear, why don't we all go over to Spain as soon as they are settled? We can all enjoy a family holiday. Will that be all right, Jane?"
"That sounds lovely; we can't wait, can we, Ben?"
"No, we can't, any one is welcome to come over to visit us."
"Good, that's settled then. Once we are settled we are thinking about getting a dog, it would give us a chance to do some walking; there are lots of unwanted dogs."
"That's nice, dear," mum said. "What breed are you thinking about?"
"Oh, a lovely Spaniel I think, I am looking forward in seeing him."
"Now then, any one for tea and you all will try some of my cake I made yesterday."
"Yes, please, mum, that will be lovely. Do you want any help?"
"No, thanks, I can manage it."
Soon it was time to leave; mum was trying to keep them all for a bit longer, she did not like saying goodbye but Jane told her she would come back another day, and take her out to dinner. She said she was looking forward to that; in the end she let them go. When Jane got home the house felt lovely and warm. Ben went to get his pipe and slippers while Jane went to put the kettle on.
"Still thirsty, dear?" Ben said.
"Yes, I have been like it all day today."
"Oh, I hope you are not getting a cold again.
"I don't think so," said Jane. "I think I will have an early night, it might shake it off."
The following morning they woke up late go: "Goodness me! Is that the time? We have not slept this late for a long time."
"No, we haven't. I think it will do us good."
"Right, the turn for tea today is yours, I think" said Jane."
"Oh, you would say that," said Ben laughing. "What do you want for breakfast, dear?
"Cereals and toast, please; my turn tomorrow."
Off went Ben to sort out the breakfast, Jane was dressed and seemed quite bright.
"A good night's sleep has done you good, dear," said Ben. "Properly you have been overdoing it a bit, but now that we have sold the house you can take it easy a bit. Why don't you give Joe a ring and do some shopping, have a girls day out?"
"Good idea, I'll give her a ring now and see if she is free. Hello, Joe, Jane here, what are you doing today?"
"Oh, hello, Jane. I was just thinking about you."
"Oh, were you Joe?"

"I was just wondering what you are doing today."
"Do you fancy a bit of shopping? We could go to that new shopping precinct, I haven't been to it yet."
"Oh, haven't you? It's lovely; they have made a park way where you can sit and enjoy your sandwiches and on a sunny day the birds come and eat your bread, if you let them. OK, what time shall we say, about 2.30 will be alright?"
"No problem, see you shortly, bye for now."
"Everything alright, dear?" Ben asked.
"Yes, I am meeting her about 2, it will make a nice change. What are you going to do?"
"Don't worry about me, I'll find something to do, have a lovely afternoon, dear."
"Do we need any more shopping, Ben?"
"No, I don't think so, dear, don't worry about anything like that, it's your afternoon off, remember."
"OK, dear."
After breakfast Jane went to get ready: "Well, dear, I'm off, see you soon."
When she arrived at her friend's house she was ready to go; usually she took ages, but today was different.
"Gosh, ready on time" said Jane laughing.
"Now, don't get cheeky or I shall not buy you dinner."
"Anyway I thought it was my treat."
"Well, soon you are on to pastures new, so I thought I would treat you just this once."
"That's very kind of you buts there's no need really."
"We will say no more about it. Are we going in my car or yours?"
"Oh, yours, please, I don't feel like driving today."
"OK, that's no problem, Jane, just let me get the car keys and then we will be off."
Soon they were on their way; it didn't take long before they were there. It looked quite busy.
"Why is it so busy?" asked Jane. "Oh, look, that's the reason: the sales are on, and they have a band playing in the square. It feels just like Christmas again." Jane was so excited, she hadn't felt like that for ages.
"I bet you are glad that the house is sold, Jane, I've never seen you like this before."
"No, it's good to have that sorted; I can relax a bit now. You must come over and visit us soon; it will be fun to show you around."
"Don't worry, we will be over like a shot, Jane, love; you're not getting rid of me that easy."
Jane laughed and said: "No, I suppose I won't. We have always been friends, haven't we?"
They brought quite a few things and then they decided to have some lunch, they were quite thirsty with all the talking they had done, but they certainly enjoyed themselves.
"Goodness! We seemed to have brought a lot," said Joe. "What will Ben say?"
"I'll worry about that when I get home," said Jane. "After all, Ben did say *go out and enjoy yourself* and that's what I have been doing, and now I am going to enjoy my lunch, the rest can take care of itself."

Joe laughed at her friend, she had never seen her in this mood for a long time, and it was good to see.
"That was a wonderful lunch," said Joe. "I've never enjoyed myself so much. Have you enjoyed it too?"
"Yes, I have! Thank you for the dinner, it was lovely. We must do it again soon."
"We will have to save up a bit first I think, don't you agree?"
"Yes, it would be a good idea, well let's get back."
It was a lovely drive back, Joe was a good driver. They went indoors, Joe went to make tea. Their house was always so warm and had a homely atmosphere to it; Jane remarked to Joe when she came into the room.
"Yes," said Joe. "We think so to, and I am glad you feel the same way. I don't think we shall have any problems selling this."
"Why, are you thinking of moving too?"
"Oh not for a while yet, maybe in a few years from now, when the children have grown up a bit."
"Where were you thinking of then, Joe, does Spain appeal to you then?"
"I am not sure. I think I will see how you settle in first."
"A good idea," said Jane. "Now I must be on my way, I don't like driving in the dark. I'll just give Ben a ring and tell him I am on my way."
When Jane got home Ben was in the lounge having a smoke with his pipe.
"That pipe will be the death of you yet" said Jane.
"Oh, hello, Jane. Did you have a nice time? How is Joe?"
"I can only answer one question at a time, Ben. Yes, she is fine, and yes, we had a lovely time, and Joe brought me dinner. It was so busy and there was a band playing in the park; we talk about old times and she wants to come over and see us once we are settled, will that be alright?"
"Of course, dear, it's fine by me. Now what have you been buying?"
"Oh, girl's things, you know, some things for Spain... Oh, I brought you a summer shirt; it was in the sale and I couldn't resist it."
Ben laughed, and said: "What is it with women they can't resist a good bargain?"
"Well, you did tell me to go out and enjoy myself, didn't you?"
"Yes, dear, I did, I was only joking, love."
Jane went across to him and kissed him on his forehead.
"What was that for?" said Ben.
"Nothing, dear, just felt like it," and went into the kitchen to make some tea; the phone was ringing and Jane went to answer it: "Hello," she said. "Can I help you? Oh, it's you, Mary, anything wrong? We haven't heard from you for ages."
"I am ringing to ask you if you are still interested in the bungalow."
"Yes, of course we are, we sold our house a while back, and we are almost in the last stages of completion, so we will be over to see it soon. We have booked the ferry, mum is coming with us."
"Oh, that's good, then I'll tell the owners, then we can get things moving this end. Looking forward in seeing you both soon."
"Bye for now."

"Who was that on the phone, dear?" Ben asked.
"It was Mary from Spain, dear, they are holding the bungalow for us."
"Oh, that's good, we liked that one, didn't we?"
"Yes, and it was in the right area."
"And the right price," said Ben laughing. "It seems everything is going to plan, doesn't it Jane?"
"Yes, it does. I for one can't wait."
"I know what you mean, dear, it will come soon enough. Well, I think I am off to bed."
"Alright, dear, I will be up soon. Do you want a nightcap?"
"No, thanks, I shall be asleep soon."
"I'll say good night then".
They were up bright and early; Jane made a pot of tea, and took one up to Bill.
"Thank you, dear," he said. "I was getting thirsty. I will be up soon."
"Don't worry, there is no rush. What do you want for breakfast?"
"Oh, a piece of toast and marmalade would be OK. We will be off to sunny Spain in a few weeks, and when we come back we should be ready to leave for good."
"Yes, it's getting close now. Mum is quite excited about it, I think she would like to come out and live with us too. It's a pity dad isn't so keen, still, who knows? He might change his mind you know."
"Yes, there is that," said Ben. "Now, how about my breakfast? I shall have to go and fetch my paper soon. I like a good read in the mornings."
Jane laughed: "Yes, I do know, Ben, and don't forget tobacco for you pipe, dear."
"Oh, thanks for reminding me, I almost forgot."
"Here's you toast and tea; you know, the weather isn't too bad today, I might go for a walk this afternoon."
"That's nice, dear, it will do you good. Now I must go and fetch my paper, Jane, bye for now."
When Ben came back Jane had washed up, and put away the pots. Since the house viewing she had sort of got used to being tidy, and now it had become a habit, and habits die hard as they say. In the afternoon she went for a walk, the sun shone but there was a northwest wind, and she pulled up the collar of her coat and wrapped her scarf around her neck, then she felt warmer. She reached the park and went to feed the ducks; there was one favourite she liked, it was brown and white with a dark beak. It was rather cheeky, always first in the queue, she will really miss coming there, that was where she did all her think in, but she had made her choice and she had to act on it. Soon it was time to go, she promised she would come and say her goodbye before she went. It was a nice walk home but the wind was getting stronger now, and she shivered a little, she was glad to be getting indoors. Ben was in the lounge reading his paper and of course his pipe. Jane loved the smell of his pipe, the warmth from the fire was welcoming.
"Oh, hello, dear, had a good walk? My you have some rosy cheeks, it's put some colour into them."
"Yes, it was a good walk. I've been to feed the ducks; they are lovely, I shall miss them."

"Well, I suppose they have ponds and ducks in Spain, you know, dear."
"Yes, I know, but these are my special ones."
Ben laughed: "You will get some more over there, dear, I'm sure. Now come and put your feet up and sit by the fire, you look cold. I will go and make us a nice cup of tea and a piece of that nice fruit cake mum made."
"Oh, that would be lovely."
Jane got out her book, when Ben came in with the tea he found her fast asleep. *Well, would you believe it? That walk must have tired her out, I can't wait to get her over to Spain, she looks warn out, bless her*, he said to himself. He looked out of the window and saw it was raining, Jane just got home in time. It was good to her to relax a bit, next month they will be in Spain, for Ben it couldn't come soon enough. Ben went to put the meat in the slow oven, then he started to do the vegetables, he thought he would surprise Jane in having the dinner ready when she woke up. She looked dead to the world; he lit his pipe and made himself a cup of coffee, and read some more of his paper. He could hear the rain belting down against the window. *Oh, what an horrible afternoon it's turned out to be*, he said to himself, *I am glad we are not out in this, the fire is very welcoming on days like this, I shall miss it, it looks so homely I think.*
"Oh, did you say something dear?"
"Oh, good, you're awake. I will go and make you some coffee, or would you rather have tea?"
"No, coffee would be fine, thanks."
Off he went, while he was there he checked on the dinner, it did smell good that slow oven was worth its wait in gold.
"Here you are, Jane, coffee and a biscuit to go with it."
"Oh, you spoil me, Ben."
"If I can't spoil my wife now and then when can I?"
Jane laughed: "You are a dear, oh, and that dinner smells good to. Hark at that rain, I won't be surprised if we get a thunder storm, it feels quite heavy. How long have I been asleep, Ben?"
"Oh, about 2 hours, I say"
"No, never that long, I haven't done that in ages."
"Well, you must have needed it, dear, it won't do you any harm."
"Oh, I don't suppose it will, love, now how about that dinner? I am starving.
"It won't be long now, give it another half an hour, and I will go and sort it."
"In that case, I think I will go and get a quick shower."
"OK, love, I will call you when it's ready."
"Thanks, Ben, you're a dear." She went over to kiss him.
"Now what was that for?"
"Oh, you know!"
Well, Ben didn't know, but it made him smile just the same. The rain had quieted down a bit but it still looked a bit black over the east. He but some more coal on the fire, and drew the curtains: it looked really cosy. When Jane came down dinner was ready; it certainly smelt good, they were always hungry these days. Ben

found some more wine. *This will finish the meal off nicely*, he thought to himself. Jane came down from her shower, she looked really refreshed and looking very happy.
"What are you smiling at, Mr. Jones?" she said.
"Oh, nothing dear, come and get your dinner. I have found some wine to go with it."
"My word we are going to town tonight."
"Well, it's such a horrible evening outside, this makes up for it, don't you think?"
"It certainly does," said Jane and she gave him one of her warm smiles. "Well, that was a very good dinner, thank you very much."
"That's alright, it's your turn tomorrow, dear."
"OK by me, now shall we have a nice cuppa in the lounge? It's a shame to waste that lovely warm fire."
"OK, dear, just getting my pipe."
"Oh, you and that pipe."
"It's the only thing I enjoy that doesn't cost a lot."
"Alright, dear, I will let you of this once."
"All lovely, it's hard to choose. Well, just think this time next week we will be house hunting."
"Don't forget we have to go and sign some more papers before we go."
"Oh, that's right, I had forgotten all about that, Jane! Good job you remembered."
"Well, I don't think they would have forgotten it." They watched a bit of television.
"Not much on tonight, Ben, I think I will have an early night. I might as well make the most of this quiet period, soon it will be all go."
Ben laughed and said: "You can say that again. Have you finished that book you were reading?"
"Yes, I read it last week, it was very good. I am on another one now."
"You are beginning to be a proper book worm."
"Well, it's good to keep the brain active; you ought to try it sometime."
"Oh, my paper's good enough for me, thanks. Do you want a nightcap bringing up?"
"Thanks, that would be nice, and a biscuit, please."
Ben went up later; Jane was hard into her book. "Here you are, dear, lovely hot cocoa."
"Oh, thank you, Ben. Are you coming to bed now?"
"Yes, dear, I am, let me brush my teeth, then I'll be with you." Soon he was by her side. "Isn't lovely? You feel like a hot water bottle."
"And you feel like an iceberg."
They had their nightcap and snuggled down to sleep. Soon it was morning, the birds were singing.
"It's going to be a nice day today, dear" said Ben.
"Eh, what did you say?" said she rubbing her eyes.
"Come on, sleepy head, waky, waky."
"Whose turn for tea?"
"Yours I think."
"Oh, you're out of bed, you do it?"

"OK, I shan't be long."
Jane went to the bathroom and had a quick shower, that always did the trick. When Ben came up, he said: "My, that was quick! I thought you would still be in bed."
"No, I thought I would be first in line for the bathroom, you always take to long."
Soon they were both dressed and ready to face the day. It was going to be a sad day and an exciting day, they were to sign the house over to the other buyers, they were moving in around Christmas time, as there had been a hold up on the chain, so it gave them plenty of time to find a house in Spain. They had some shopping to do, rather than have dinner late they decided to have it out. So they would be out most of the day, it made a change to be out together, and they still had a few plans to make, Jane always got excited, Ben had some very good ideas. When they arrived at the estate agents, they were made very welcome, once the papers were signed they felt relieved and happy, at last they were on their way. A few weeks later they went to pick mum up, said goodbye to every one and they were on their way. Mum was so excited she talked non-stop till they got to their first toilet stop, and a coffee break. They had a sandwiches and a lovely fruit cake.
"That was nice, Jane, but not as good as mine."
"Oh, mother," said Jane. "I hope you are not going to say that on all Spanish food."
"No, dear, I was just comparing the cake, that's all!"
"Oh, good, that's all right then. Shall we get back to Ben? He has been very patient up to now, we don't want to spoil things. Are you going to have a sleep now? We have still got a long way to go, you know."
"Yes, I think I will dear, I didn't think it was this far."
"We have even further to go once we get onto the Spanish boarder, but once we are there it will be fun."
"Hello you two, my, you have been a long time."
"Well, you know mother."
"When two women get together, yes I do know. Are we ready now then?"
"Yes, dear, I think we are."
Off they went again, a few more hours they should be at the dock, it was a sunny day and quite a pleasant drive down. Now the two women were asleep, life wasn't so bad after all. There was no hold ups for quite a while until they were near Portsmouth and the girls woke up.
"Goodness, that was a long sleep, are you alright Ben?"
"I was till you woke up, yes. I'm fine, thanks; did you have a good sleep?"
"The car is so quiet you hardly know you're moving!" said mum. "How long will it be before were there?"
"Oh, it shouldn't be to long, I would say about another hour, mum," said Ben. "Why, do you want another stop?"
"No, I think I can wait a bit longer, dear."
"If you can't, let me know. I think there is a toilet at the port."
"Oh, good, I think I will have a little sleep."
When Jane turned to look at her mum, she was fast asleep. "You wouldn't think butter wouldn't melt in her mouth, would you, Ben?"

"I can't see her very well, dear, I am driving."
"Sorry, dear, mind if I have forty winks?"
"Not at all," said Ben. *Anything for a quite life*, he said to himself and soon it was all quite. An hour went by and soon he was coming into the port.
"We are here now, so if you want to freshen up now is your chance."
"Oh, that was the longest journey I have ever had."
"Well, I am afraid it's not over yet, we still have the other side to do."
"Goodness, I had forgotten all about that."
Ben had to go and sort out the tickets and cabin numbers for the ship.
"Doesn't it look big," said Jane. "I hope we are near each other."
"I'm sure Ben will see we are. He's a good caring man, once you get to Spain he will take care of you."
"Oh, here he comes now looking pleased with himself."
"That's all settled, we are not far from each other which is good."
"Oh, well, Ben; when do we sail?"
"Not long now, dear, another hour and we should be on our way."
"Good," said mum getting rather excited. "Is there anywhere where we can have some coffee and a sandwich?"
"Yes," said Ben. "There's a small canteen near the office, they are quite reasonable: we can leave the car here, as no one is going anywhere yet, so let's go and eat shall we?"
It was quite warm in the room, you could see the ships in the dock, some big, some small, it was all very interesting and the time went by so quickly. Soon they got word that they were on the move, they could see their ship. My, wasn't it big? There were lots of cars, all rearing to go.
"We had better get back to the car, Jane, we don't want to hold any one up."
So off they went; soon they were on deck, they took their luggage out of the car and went in search of their cabin. The girls were getting very excited, Jane spotted theirs first.
"Look it's not to small, as we thought it might be, Ben."
"It's quite a good size, I'll better go and find mine."
So of he went, the girls were alone, mum hugged her daughter.
"What was that for?"
"Just felt like it, dear," she said. "I am very happy for both of you. I know Ben will take care of you out in Spain."
"I am sure he will, mum."
Just then Ben came and popped his head round the corner: "Are you girls ready for dinner? I am starving."
"We're almost ready, Ben."
"Five minutes then" said Ben. They found their way to the dining room: "Oh, isn't this lovely, Jane? Now the holiday has really begun."
Once they had had their meal they went to explore the ship. They sat down near one of the seats; they could see for miles around, someone was speaking over the tannoy: In one hour time the dolphins will be coming alongside the ship; if you want to see them go up to the second deck, it's a sight not to be missed.

"Oh, let's go up, Jane, dear, and have a look."
"OK, mum; are you coming Ben?"
"No, dear, I will stay here and mind the seat, you go if you like."
"OK, we won't be long."
Ben was on his own. Isn't this peaceful?, he said to himself; it was quite a long drive and all of a sudden he felt quite tired. His coffee untouched, he felt the ship's movement and he could hear the waves hitting the side of the ship. It didn't bother him too much; when the girls came back he was fast asleep.
"Look at Ben, that drive must have worn him out. Weren't the dolphins lovely, mum?"
"I got some really good shots to show dad back home, luckily it was a clear day."
"Shall we wake Ben up?" "I think he will be better in his cabin."
"OK," Jane said. "Come on, sleepy head, let's get you to your cabin, you will sleep better there."
So off they went, back to their cabins, sure enough Ben was soon fast asleep again.
"Shall we go and have a bit of a rest, mum? We have quite a long wait for evening meal and there is a show on in the theatre bar tonight."
"OK, dear, let me go to the bathroom first."
"There's a lovely book I want to read," said Jane. "Do you want the bottom bunk, mum?"
"Yes, please, dear. I think I will be safer in that, don't you?"
"Yes, I think you will, mum," and Jane read for a while and soon they were asleep.
An hour later they all woke up: "Goodness, I have never slept so long, what time is it?"
"Not be long before it's dinner time."
"Are you hungry?"
"Just a bit," said Jane. "I am looking forward to the show. I wonder what Ben is doing. Oh, here he his now, I bet he is hungry too."
"Hello you two. What have you been up to?"
"We have had quite a long sleep and we have done some reading. The dolphins were lovely, Ben, it's a shame you missed them. You will be able to see them on the way back though. Now, how about some dinner?"
Soon they were all seated at their tables.
"Oh, this looks good too," mum said. "I shall soon put on some more weight."
"Well, you are on holiday, mum, it will do you good," she carried on with her meal.
"This wine tastes good," said mum. "I suppose in Spain you have it with every meal, as it's so cheap."
"That's right, mum, you do. *Sangría* isn't too bad either; it's still warm even at this time of the year..."
"Well, has every one finish their meal, as we have to get ready for the show?"
"OK, Ben, let's go and get sorted."
Soon they made their way back to the cabin.
"This will look alright, Jane, don't you think?"
"Yes, mum, it looks lovely. Right, are we ready?"

"Coming, dear" mum said.
They made their way down to the cinema; there were lots of people there already.
"Gosh, look at the crowd, are they all going in here?" said mum.
"Yes, I think so," said Ben. "I am sure we shall get in."
Ben was right, they had a good view, and soon the show got under way. There was some singing, dancing and telling jokes; soon it was half time. Mum wanted an ice cream and Jane wanted a drink, so Ben went to fetch them, as he was at the end of the file.
"Here you are you two; hope you enjoy them."
"Thank you, Ben, we will. Oh, they're starting the second half already; they don't give you much time, do they?"
"Well, I think they need to get home and have their meals, just like us," said Jane. "Now let's sit back and enjoy the second half."
When the curtains went up the crown started to move.
"Oh, that was most enjoyable. Shall we go for a nightcap?
"Yes, why not?" said Jane.
"I am going for a beer."
"OK, Ben, we will meet you at the coffee lounge.
"It's been ages since I have been to a show it was so colourful, and the dancing was lovely."
"I enjoyed it too" said Jane.
Ben came back: "Well, wasn't that lovely? I don't usually go in for shows, but I wouldn't have missed that. Now I am off to bed; how about you, ladies, are you ready? We have a long drive tomorrow and I think we should all get an early night."
"I agree," said mum. "I am tired anyway, and I shan't be long before I will be asleep."
Off they went back to their cabin. The sea was quiet at the moment, all you could hear was the waves against the ship's side; they said goodnight to Ben and soon they were asleep. Later on they all woke up, went for a shower —that always does the trick— and they went down for breakfast. Mum liked their bacon best while Jane liked their scrambled egg and orange juice; at one o'clock they heard that the dolphins would be in the area, as it was a clear day they would get a good view of them.
"Shall we all go out and see them?" said mum.
"Why not? Ben can see them this time, can't you, Ben?"
"Yes I am looking forward to seeing them; we could take some more shots of them."
They went up to the top deck and they had some more drinks and they sat near the window, it was a lovely clear day and the sea looked as though it had a whole plain of glass on it. You couldn't wish for a better view.
"What time are we leaving the ship, Ben?"
"Oh, not till this evening; we have two more meals before we go, we stop at one of the motels for the night and then we travel down to Murcia around midday. We should be in there at 5 p.m. I have booked into the hotel where Jane stayed, they made her most welcome and now they are good friends so it made sense to stay there."
"What a very good idea! It makes things easier when you know people."
Sure enough the excitement of the dolphins brought them up to the top deck, it was a wonderful moment and they got some good shots.

These will look great on film, and the sea looks lovely too."
After all the excitement, they went to the dining room; Ben fancied some steak for his dinner while Jean and Joyce had fish. The chips were chunky which they both liked, washed down with some more coffee. Later on they went for a walk round the ship, it was really one of the most wonderful ships they had been on, and soon they would be leaving it all behind: mum would be going back by plane as driving down proved to much for her, Jean and Ben were coming back on their own. Jean and her mum went to have a lie down before their long journey, they had packed some of their things up the day before, so there wasn't much to do. They had a lovely rest; Ben came in to see them:
"Are you about ready to leave? Don't forget to have your passports ready; the weather is quite good, so there is no problem there. They will tell us when we have to go to the car, which shouldn't be long now."
"Oh good," said mum. "I am getting really excited."
"Me too," said Jane. "I can't wait till I start house hunting. I saw one that I liked, but whether Ben will like it, I don't know."
"Did I here my name mentioned?"
"Oh, hello, Ben, dear. Yes, I was just telling mum about that house I liked over there."
"Oh, yes, I saw a picture of it, didn't I? It looked alright but I would like to see it for real."
"Of course you shall, dear, there will be lots more houses to look at too. I think I can hear someone shouting about cars drivers wanted up deck. Shall we go now? Ready, mother? We're on our way at last."
It wasn't long before they reached the car. "That's our car," mum shouted.
"Alright, mum, I can see it. Now in you get and please don't make so much noise" said Ben laughing.
The cars in front were moving off, so as Ben got the all clear they were away, they were on the right road so the girls sat back to enjoy the ride.
"Can we stop for some refreshments soon?"
The sun was beaming down on them: mum had to take off her cardigan, so did Jean.
"This sun is very powerful today, is it always like this?" mum asked Jane.
"This time of the year it can be quite strong; in the summer it gets even stronger."
"Goodness, will you be able to cope with it?"
"We won't have any choice, will we?"
"You could always come home, dear" said mum.
"Maybe we will, we will have to see. It's a long way of yet. They arrived at their hotel at around 7 p.m., later than they anticipated. Mary was the first to greet them.
"Come away in," she said. "It's so good to see you again, Jane, and this is your husband and mother. Hello, Mr. Jones, I have heard so much about you all. Let me show you to your rooms. I have put the girls in this one, you can see the sea from here, and also in Ben's room too. The hotel is very quite at the moment, so you will get some rest, dinner will be served in few minutes. I am sure you will like what we have, so I will let you all get settled in."

"Thank you, Mary, we will look forward to it."
"What a nice lady, Jean, I can see why you like her. Is she Scottish? I think there is a bit in her, I can tell by her accent."
"Do you want that bed near the window, mum? There's a good view of the sea."
"I don't mind which one I have Jean, I am going to enjoy this holiday just being with my favourite daughter, and Ben, of course."
"It's nice being with you too, mum."
"Now let's go and get some dinner. I am starving as usual, Jane."
The dinning room hadn't changed much, although they had changed the decor in the lounge. The dinner was lovely, they had roast beef, for afterwards they could have either ice cream or fruit cocktail; they had ice cream which went down a treat. They had their coffee in the lounge; the sun was still shining, soon they would be able to see the sunset. It was all very nice, and so quiet all they could hear was the waves from the sea. Ben asked if he could smoke his pipe, as that was one thing he liked to do after his meal and he wasn't prepared to give that up just yet!, he said to Jane.
"That's alright dear, if that's what you want."
"What's on telly tonight, Mary? Any thing worth watching?"
"Yes, there is a documentary on wild life in Africa and how they saved the elephants."
"What time is that on?"
"Oh, about 8 p.m."
"Shall we watch it? It sounds good!"
"Why not?" said mum. "That would be lovely."
"Any one for more coffee?"
"Yes, please, Mary" mum said.
"OK, won't be a moment." When she came back Ben was asleep. "Goodness, that drive must have worn him out, he looks so peaceful."
"It was a lovely journey, but when we came over to the other side it got quite hot in the car. We had to stop for a bit of fresh air and a drink. The views were breathtaking, and we took some pictures to show dad, didn't we, Jane?"
"Yes, he will enjoy looking at them."
Ben woke up with a start and said: "Dinner was rather nice, wasn't it? The landlady is too."
"Yes, she is, dear! I think mum likes her too."
"When do we start house hunting?"
"We are meeting June the day after tomorrow."
"Where's your mum?"
"She is having a chat with Mary."
"If your mum likes her then she must be alright."
"I can't wait to show you the area, it's really nice round here. I would like somewhere a bit further in land, what do you think, Ben?"
"As long as I am with you I don't mind where it is, dear."
"Very nice of you to say so, but both of us must like it too."
"I know dear, but don't look so serious, it will all be alright in the end, I'm sure."

"I am just going to tell mum we are going for a walk."
When she saw her mum she was fast asleep on the bed, so she didn't wake her up, but went down to tell Mary if she would keep an eye on her for an hour."
"Of course, dear, I will. Do you think she will need a nightcap?"
"Oh, that would be lovely. We shan't be long any way."
Jane was so excited as she knew the area quite well and she wanted to show Ben the area where they might be living. On the way down to the sea front they meet one of the neighbours.
"Oh, hello," Jane said. "How are you?"
"Hello, Jean, it's nice to see you again. Have you moved here already?"
"No, not quite yet, but we are now seriously thinking of moving here soon. We have sold our house, back in the UK, Joan, so you will soon see a lot more of us. This is my husband, Ben."
"Hello," said Ben. "Nice to see you, do you live far from here?"
"You see that little villa just down the road? That's where I live. Come around for coffee some time, we could have it on the patio."
"We have brought mum with us this time to show her where we hope to live."
"Bring her along too, then we can have a good old chat. What do you think of the area so far, Ben?" Joan asked Ben.
"It's lovely," he said. "The houses are so cheap, and there are some lovely views too."
"We must be on our way, otherwise it will be too dark to show Ben the harbour."
"Bye for now then, see you soon."
"Look, Ben, there's a big ship in the harbour. I wonder what it is called, let's go and see."
"Mary Anne. Oh, what a lovely name, that gives me an idea about our house."
"Oh, now here we go again, you and your romantic ideas."
Jane laughed: "Some ones got to be, you know."
"Yes, dear," Ben said. "Shall we get back to the hotel now? Your mum will be wondering where we are." Ben turned around to face Jane and said: "Romantic or not I still love you, and will do everything to make you happy, darling."
"Oh, Ben, you're such a love, and I too love you. We will be OK over here, I know we will."
They kissed each other tenderly and walked back to the hotel. It was getting really cold now, but it was a clear night; when they got back in there was a roaring fire in the lounge and mum was talking to Mary. Mum looked relaxed and happy, the sleep did her good.
"Hello you two; had a good walk?"
"Yes, thanks, mum. There were some big ships in the harbour tonight, there was one called Mary Anne."
"Yes, and now Jane wants to call our house that name. What do you think, mum?"
"I think we had better find a house first, Ben. Jean was always the romantic type when she was younger, you know."
"Was she? I never knew that."
"Oh, you two give over, you are making me blush."
"Does anyone want a nightcap? I know I do, it was quite chilly out there tonight."

"I fancy a beer; is the bar open? Do you know?"
"I will go and find out for you."
So off she went; later she came back with the beer and coffee, and a few sandwiches.
"Thank you, Jane how thoughtful of you" mum said.
"What's on the box tonight, mum?"
"There is a good film on, later it's a weepy one."
"Oh, in that case I shall go and have an early night and watch football. They won't mind me taking my beer with me?"
"I shouldn't think so, dear, as long as you don't take your pipe with you," mum said smiling at him. "Night."
"Night then, see you in the morning, mum."
"Alright, dear, bye for now." Jane went to put some more coal on the fire. "Doesn't this room feel cosy?" Jean said.
"Yes, it does," said mum. "You wouldn't think you would need it in Spain."
"It does get cold at night, mum," said Jane. "And you get some lovely sunsets too."
Soon it was time for the film to start, and sure enough it was a real weepy; lucky there was some tissues handy. After a few hours both had red eyes.
"I think that was one of the weepiest films I have seen in a long time," mum said. "I am now in need of a nightcap. How about you, Jane?"
"I fancy a tot of whisky."
"Is there any sherry?"
"You're in luck, here you are; that will make you sleep, mum."
"Yes, it will, dear. What did Ben think of the area, Jane, did he like it?"
"Yes, he did, mum, and I think we have chosen the area now. We are not far from the shops and doctors, mum, so I think we will try and find somewhere near here.
Jean put the guard around the fire and went in search of Mary, who was in the office.
"We are off to bed now, Mary. I have seen to the fire, and all is safe. Tomorrow we shall be out for lunch but be in for supper, is that alright with you?"
"Yes, dear, that will be OK as long as I know. I hope you find what you are are looking for."
"Thank you, Mary, I am sure we will. Good night to you" and they both went off to bed.

House searching

They awoke early to a glorious sunny day.
"Mum, make sure you put lots of sun cream on, and a hat chimed in, Ben."
"A good idea, I think I will put one on too. What time are we meeting June?"
"In about 2 hours time, so we have time for breakfast."
"Yes," said Jane. "We have. First we are going into Torrevieja and we will properly have coffee somewhere."

"Isn't it exciting?" said mum. "Your very own place in the sun."
"Now's the time to buy," said Ben. "They have gone down a lot in price, which makes it easier for us to choose."
"Well, there are certainly lots to choose from, dear," said Jane. "I think this area will be good for us too. Let's take our coffee out in the patio."
Ben got out his pipe and mum started to read, while Jane was busy looking at some houses and bungalows. There were certainly some nice ones about, she thought to herself. Soon it was time to go, camera in hand they walked to the car; it was a lovely red one with open roof and plenty of room. Mum felt like royalty, the lady was friendly and full of information.
"Well, it is her job," said Ben. "So she should be OK".
The bungalows were lovely and spacious, the houses were even bigger.
"Would we be able to have another look at one or two again?" said Ben.
"Of course, you can take as long as you like, you don't have to decided straight away. This is just to get you started, so you can see what you are getting for your money. After all, it is a long term adventure, one not to be taken lightly."
"No, your quite right, it isn't" mum said.
The next day they went back to one of the bungalows they liked and put down a deposit, they were very excited, and so was Mary.
"Hurray! They said you are not very far from us, Jane."
"We can go out for coffee and go to that nice park we like."
Mum was very quiet when they got back into the lounge.
"Are you alright, mum?" Jane asked. "Only you have gone very quite."
"I am so pleased that you have decided on that bungalow. Now it's all happening so fast, soon I shall be leaving for home."
"Don't forget, mum, we have to return home to put things in order; it will be another month at least before things are finalized." She went over to give her mum a big hug. "You are OK about us moving over here, aren't you?"
"Yes, dear, I am just being selfish."
"No, you're not; you're just being mum, and I won't have you any other way. You're one of the best mums in the world and we will get you a laptop so you can keep in touch."
"Oh, that's a good idea. I feel better already, so no more tears."
"Come and have a drink with us!"
"OK, dear, I will be a long in a minute."
They were all sitting round the fire, when the phone rang.
"Hello," said Mary. "Who's speaking?"
"Eh, could I speak to Joyce, please?"
"Yes, just one moment; I will go and fetch her. Joyce, there is a phone call for you."
"Oh, thank you, Mary, I will go and answer it."
When she came back she was all smiles!
"Anything the matter?" said Jane.
"No, just the opposite," said Joyce. "Dad's got the all clear about his cancer scare, he has to visit his doctor next week for some tablets."

"That's good news," said Ben. "Now you can really start to enjoy the rest of the holiday. You are naughty though, mum. You shouldn't have kept that from us."
"Well, I didn't want to ruin your happy time. I don't think you would have come to Spain if you had known."
"All the same, mum, you should have told us."
"Yes, I see that now, but he is OK and that's all that matters, isn't it?"
"Yes, mum you're right," said Ben. "Now are we having dinner tonight? I am starving." They all laughed.
"Ben and his stomach" said Jane.
"Don't forget his pipe" said mum.
"Oh, come you two, less of the teasing, time to eat."
It's time to go down to the dining room, as usual, it was a lovely meal.
"I think we shall be eating here quite a lot," said Ben to Mary. "You always put on a good meal."
"I have just heard your dad's good news about his cancer scare."
"Yes, it was," said Ben. "We don't want to her any more about that, do we, Jean?"
"No, Mary, we don't, so please don't say any more to mum, let her enjoy the rest of her stay here."
"Of course I understand, dear. Would you like more coffee?"
"Oh, yes, please, Mary, that would nice."
Off she went to make the coffee. In the afternoon they all decided to go for a walk along the beach. It was a pleasant afternoon, just a little breeze coming of the sea, there was some people around walking their dogs, children playing in the sand.
"That's what we will get, when we get settled," said Jane suddenly, as neither had spoken a word for a long time.
"Well, where did that come from?" said Ben.
"I just thought about it, that's all. I was seeing those people with their dogs, they look as though they are having such fun... Can we get one then?" said Jane.
"Yes, dear, we can when we get settled. Now how about an ice cream? There's a van over there, shall we go and see?"
"Yes, please," mum said, feeling like a child again. "That cornet looks lovely, I think I will have one of those"
"Why not?" said Jane. "What are you going to have, Ben?"
"I might have a waver, then we can go and have a coffee somewhere."
The man who was serving the ice creams told them there was a good coffee shop not far from here.
"Oh," they all said. "That's good, we will go and see if we can find it."
Not far from the coffee shop there was a lovely park; when Jane saw it she jumped up and down, feeling very excited and feeling like a 4 year old again.
"Jane, what ever is the matter with you, dear?"
"Look over there, by the tree there is a peacock and some squirrels."
"Well, you have seen them before surely."
"Yes, I know I have, mum, but not it this environment, and they have there own space to do what they like in. Also it's not far from us, we can come here when ever we want."

"Of course you can," said Ben. "We can also have a picnic too. It's going to be lovely living here."
So off they went, found a bench and had their ice cream. It was late in the afternoon so they made their way back to the hotel, as they made their way back they saw a wonderful sight.
"Oh, look at those little ducklings walking along by the side of the road, and the cars are going slow for them."
"Well, I think they are protected species" said Ben.
"Oh, are they?" Jane said. "I am not at all surprised to hear you say that."
"No, neither am I" said mum smiling.
"I would like to take a photograph of them, that would be great," said Ben. "Are we ready to go back now? I think it's supper time." said Ben.
So they made their way back.
"Had a good afternoon everyone?"
"Yes, it's been lovely, Mary."
"Do you often go to the park? It's so lovely down there and lots of wild life which I love."
"We know that, don't we, Ben?"
"We certainly do," said Ben. "She was so excited it was as though we had another child with us."
"Well, I can understand why she felt like that, that's how I feel sometimes," said Mary, winking at Jane as she spoke. Now come along in, I have a lovely supper for you all. Do you want drinks first?"
"Oh, yes, please, Mary, that would be nice."
They went into the lounge, the sun was still beaming though it had been a very warm evening.
"We have roast duck and lame steak beef. Does that sound OK, Ben?"
"Yes, it sounds lovely. June I have steak?"
"I will have duck" said mum and Jane asked it too. "I might go and have a little lie down, that walk's made me more tired than I thought, will you call me for dinner please, Jane?"
"Of course, mother, have a good rest now, see you soon."
You could smell the dinner all round the hotel and every one was saying how good the food was here, this time of the year it was always full. When Jane looked out of the bedroom window the sun was just setting in the sky, it was full of colour and she went to get the camera, it was too good to miss. She couldn't wait to see the play-back when they got home, of course she looked at the calendar and sign, not long to go now before they had to go home. She had to remember to check the airline for mum, she thought. They came down for dinner, the dining room was full, with a good atmosphere, they were all talking about the sunset, they hadn't seen one like that for quite a while.
"It looks as though it will be a very warm day tomorrow" said John, who was next door to Ben's bedroom. They got quite friendly and promised to write when they got back to the UK.

"Yes, I think it will be, I wonder if there will be any coach trips."
"Could enquire with Mary, they might even do one from the hotel."
They checked on the board, sure enough there was one going to Valencia, so they booked it for the following day. That afternoon they all went for a walk along the beach, the sun shone and the sea was quite calm. Ben said: "I hope the sea will be like this when we go home."
"Yes, so do I," said Jane. "Are you sure you want to go home by plane, mum?"
"Oh, yes, Jane, I do," said mum. "I can't wait to get back to dad, and show him the pictures we have."
"I hope he likes where we will be living."
"I am sure he will, it is such a nice area and there are lots of English people around it."

The day trip

They all woke up early, sure enough the sun was still shining, it looked like it was going to be a wonderful day. Mary suggested that they should take some refreshments with them; there was plenty of restaurants around so they wouldn't go hungry.
The coach pulled up just outside the hotel, there was quite a lot of people going to Benidorm, well, why not? It was too good a day to miss, and of course mum had to go back to dad soon, she was going on ahead of them, they were to follow in a few days time.
They arrived in Benidorm around 12 p.m., they could have lunch at any restaurant of their choice providing they were back with the coach at 2 p.m.
After lunch they had a look in all the tourist shops, bought some things to take home, and had another coffee not far from the coach park, so as not to be late back.
The day was going really well when all of a sudden the coach came to a complete stop. The driver shook his head and turn to his passengers. "I think I had better get on to the bus company and see if they can provide us with some transport to carry us onto our destination, we are not far from it actually, but this old bus is not going anywhere. We were going to take you on a boat across to another island where there's a lot of wild life for you to see, and possibly take pictures. Anyway I'll phone through and see what they can come up with. Don't worry, folks, help is at hand: they are going to send us one of Benidorm's buses, so we will be going after all."
"Oh, good," said Jane. "I would have been disappointed not to have gone there."
"Me too" said mum and everyone agreed. While they waited, the driver went to get them all a drink; there was a coffee bar not far from where they were parked, and it was free.
After about an hour they were on their way, and the sun was still high in the sky, it wasn't long before they were there and the view was breathtaking to say the least.

Soon the cameras were out in force clicking away, there was all the wild life you can imagine, and the sea was as calm as a lillypond. All too soon it was time to head for shore as it was getting late. This bus was their transport to home, it wasn't quite so luxurious as there old one, but at least they weren't walking, and it didn't really matter what time they got home, and they all agreed on that. Some were having a good old sing song while others had a little nod, Jane's mum was asleep long before they reach the first town. Not far behind her was Bill, so Jane sat back and enjoyed the ride. An hour or 2 later they were at their hotel, Jane had to wake them both up.
"Goodness me, you two have had a long sleep. The day must have worn you out. I hope you will sleep tonight." They both laughed and said they would, they promise.
"Never mind as long as you both enjoyed your day out."
"Oh, thank you, we did, didn't we, Ben?"
"It was nice I didn't have to drive."
"That's what I thought," said Jane. "It gave you a chance to see the views."
"It certainly did, thank you love. Now I am off to bed, are you coming up?"
"In a while, dear, I'll get us a nightcap. Want one, mum?"
"Yes, please, dear. Then I think I will go up too."
They all woke up quite early, it was to be mum's last day with them. They weren't quite sure what they were going to do. The day before was quite tiring, someone mentioned a picnic on the beach.
"That's a good idea," said mum. "I can take my book and umbrella and have a swim in the sea, then later a nice quite read."
It wasn't long before everything was ready to put in the car, it wasn't far to the beach, and it was such a sunny day, the birds were singing a merry song. When they arrived at the beach it was alive with holiday makers, some were having a barbecue, others were swimming. The umbrellas were all colours, it was a wonderful sight to see, truly picturesque scene. They found a good spot not far from the hotel so they had access to toilet facilities, and they settled down to a quiet afternoon relaxing, not saying much, but each had their own thoughts. Soon it was time to pack up and go home. When they arrived at the hotel, Mary was waiting for them: "You have a visitor waiting for you, Jane."
"Oh, who is it?"
"It's the lady from the properties office; I put her in my office for you."
"Thank you, I will go and see her, I hope it's not bad news."
"Do you want me to come with you, Jane" asked Ben, seeing the worried look on her face. He knew how much she had her heart set on the bungalow they were going to buy, still he was to find out soon enough.
"No thanks," said Jane. "I will be better to go and see her myself, thanks all the same, love."
"OK, then I will go and get mum and me some coffee. I wonder what's for dinner tonight, I'm starving."
Ben went into the kitchen to ask Mary about dinner and also to add some special drinks for their table as it was to be mum's last night with them. The dinner sounded good, he couldn't wait. He went upstairs for a shower and change, he had enjoyed

his afternoon with his wife and mother in law. She was such a lovely person he wished he could get them to move with them to Spain, but it was such a big move for them that he didn't think they were ready for that commitment in any case.
When Jane came back form the meeting with June, all smiles on her face, Ben knew he didn't need to have worried after all, but you can never tell how these things go.
Jane went to find Ben: "Everything's all right, love."
"What did she say?"
"Good news, Ben, the owners are moving out next Friday, and they are leaving all the stuff in the house, which is good, as I did like it all when I saw it, didn't you, Ben?"
"Yes, I did, Jane. It will mean we won't have to bring over much from the UK. Now we can start planning things quickly."
"I must go and tell mum, she will be happy for us."
Mum was already in the dining room, seeing Jane with a big smile on her face told all.
"That's wonderful, Jane, you will be over here sooner than you can say Jack Robinson. I am sure dad will be pleased too. I am going to phone him tonight, so I will tell him the good news, we shall have to arrange a leaving party for you, dear."
"That would be lovely, mum," said Ben. "You are the best mother-in-law any man could wish for." He went over and gave her a hug.
"Oh, go away with you, as long as you take care of my daughter I will be quite content."
As usually the dinner was lovely, and the surprise bubbly went down a treat too.
"Well, you two this is it, here's to you both and hope all your dreams will come true."
"Thank you, mum, that's very kind of you. Don't forget when you get home to dad say hi for us and we will be home soon."
They retired to the lounge and talked non-stop for ages, poor old Ben fell asleep feeling quite content with the world now they were on their way at last.
All of them went to bed feeling very happy, they had been a wonderful one.

The day of mum departure

They all woke up early and had breakfast, mum brought down her suitcase and bag, Ben borrowed Mary's car to take them to the airport. Mum was sorry to say goodbye but she knew it wasn't for long, in two weeks they would be home again. She felt happy knowing that the pair of them were about to change their lives forever. When she finally said goodbye, she boarded the plane with a happy heart. It was a good flight home, about two hours. Dad was there waiting for her; he looked well, and was happy to see her. She gave him a hug and said it was lovely to see him, and that he was looking so well after his cancer scare, still that's all behind them then, they hoped.

Joyce talked non-stop all the way home.
"It sounds as though you have had a good time, my dear."
"Oh, yes, Ben and I got bonded very well, he is such a lovely man, Tom, so down to earth, and loves Jane very much. We haven't any problems there. I knew they were meant for each other when I saw Ben.
"Oh, you are a true romantic, Joyce, love, and I love you for it."
"I know you do and so are you, my love. What have we for supper? I am hungry."
"Well, I thought as it was your first night home we would go out for a meal just this once."
"Now who's being romantic? Which restaurant are we going to, then?"
"I have booked into The Royal, your favourite."
"My goodness, we are pushing the boat out, aren't we?"
"Well, why not dear? We haven't been out much lately."
Soon they were home, everywhere looked lovely, there were even fresh flowers in the vases.
"Oh, Tom, the place looks lovely and the flowers, they smell gorgeous too, thank you, dear." And gave him a big kiss, something she hadn't done for a while. Tom went red, and went into the kitchen to make the tea: that's always a welcoming gesture.
An hour later they were sitting in their favourite restaurant having their meal, when all of a sudden someone came and tapped Joyce on her shoulder.
"Goodness me, am I seeing things."
"Yes, I thought it was Joyce, you do look well and you Tom. Have you been on holiday? It's it alright if I join you both? I haven't seen you for such a long time."
Joyce and Tom looked at each other, thinking who on earth, then, suddenly, bingo! It came to them: this tall handsome man was a friend who used to work with them in the army office, in Malta. Tom was a sargent and Mary worked as a driver at the same army camp, they hadn't seen this man for at least twenty years. He sat himself down and ordered a light meal, talking non-stop. They found out he was staying in the small hotel not far from where they lived. Would it be OK to visit them sometime? He gave them his number, and he would be in touch.
"Well, I never," said Tom. "I thought this was going to be a quiet meal just the two of us and look how it's turned out, quite extraordinary. What do you say, Joyce?"
Joyce was still trying to figure out who he was. She thought it may come tonight in bed, still it was quite a pleasant evening after all. When they arrived home the answering machine was bleeping away. Tom went to check it, as thought it was from Jane and Ben, wanting to know if mum had arrived home safely. He went back to tell Joyce who it was.
"That was nice of them dear."
They went up to bed. Tom was feeling life was certainly on the up, here he was, with his lovely wife back home and his caring family, what a lucky man he was!
In the morning Joyce wanted to go downtown to get the films developed, so she could show them to Tom.
"OK, dear, why not? I can't wait to see them."

So after breakfast they set off. Lucky they found a good parking space which wasn't far from the town center. Lots of people about, some they knew and they asked Joyce if she had a good holiday, they all thought the rest had done her good, and Tom had to agree, well, he did, didn't he? When they finally got to the shop Tom took the film, and the man told them to come back in an hour. So of course they had to go for a coffee, and still people kept coming up to talk to them.
"Do you know, Tom? If we were to leave the UK, we would be truly missed. I have only been away a few weeks, and it seems people have missed me."
"That's true, dear, look how long it has taken us just to get some prints developed."
"Talking of films, shouldn't we get back to the shop before it closes?"
"Yes, dear, your quite right, we should."
So off they went, but they waited till they got home before looking at them over a cup of tea. There was so many *ahs* and *ohs* Tom said they were very good photographs. In the selection one was the ducks, he thought they should be sent to a nature magazine, they might even be used on a calendar.
"Oh, Tom, do you think really they are that good?"
"I honesty think so, love."
"Well I never fancy that, wait till I tell Jane and Ben, they will be pleased."
"Yes, dear, I am sure they will. Now, then what's for dinner, love?"
"Just let me look in the freezer, I think pork chops are in the order of the day, don't you think?"
Joyce took the chops out of the freezer and the vegetables, peeled the potatoes ready for dinner later.
Tom went to phone Jane about the photographs, they thought it was a good idea. They asked if mum had settled down.
"Oh, yes" said Tom. "It's as though she hasn't been away."
"Good to hear she's OK, we will talk in a few days time, bye for now."
Dad put the phone back on the receiver and went in search of Joyce, who was preparing dinner.
"OK, love," she said, not looking up.
"Yes, dear, she was pleased to hear about the photographs, she said to let them know when they will be on the calendar and they could save her one."
"Of course we can, no problem. Now let's get on with the dinner, another 2 hours should be about right."
"In that case I am going into the garden. Do you want any fresh vegetable?"
"That will be lovely, dear."
The morning went by quickly and soon they were sitting at the table enjoying their meal with a glass of wine, a present from Spain.
"This wine tastes good dear, do they drink a lot of it in Spain?"
"Yes, dear, too much I am afraid."
"That can't be possible" said Tom.
"I wonder what they are doing now" said Joyce.
"Up to no good, I'll be bound," Tom said laughing. "Now their mother's gone back who knows what they get up to."

"It doesn't do them any harm to have some fun, they will have their work cut out when they start moving I think. Let's have coffee in the garden; it's such a lovely afternoon."
"Yes, what a good idea! Then I can have a look at the pictures again."
"I shall put them in my holiday snap book which I brought in Spain. They do have some nice things over there, I bet Jane will get her bungalow looking lovely."
"Yes, I bet she will, any more coffee while I am up?"
"No, thanks, dear, I am OK."
"Then I shall go and sort out that bare patch in the vegetables plot."
"OK, dear, I will just finish this, then I will get washed up."

The day of the departure

This was the day they had been waiting for.

The day was warm and sunny with a slight breeze; mum was doing her bit making cool drinks and sandwiches. Mum and dad were trying to keep cheerful, but soon they knew that by the end of the day they had to say good bye to them. Feeling that this is what they had to do. It was not that far away, two hours by plane, it wasn't as though they wouldn't see them again.
At around 6 p. m. they were on their way, they had to meet the boat in Portsmouth that evening; they were on the boat for 2 days. Jane said she would phone them on the boat once they were in dock. Mum finished the rest of the cleaning, and shut the door for the last time, sighing to herself, thinking already of them there on the boat.
"Everything alright, dear," said Tom.
"Yes, everything's alright," replied Joyce. "Can we go out for a meal tonight? I don't feel like cooking."
"I had thought of that, love, and I have booked a table at your favourite restaurant, it's been a very tiring day for us all. "
"Oh, love, thank you, you are a darling."
"We will have no more tears, everything will be OK, you will see."
"Yes, I know it will. I am just being silly."
"No, you're not, you're just being like any other mother would be. Once they are settled in we will go and visit them, will that be all right?"
"Now about that meal, I am starving" Joyce laughed.
"That's better," said Tom. "Go and get changed, and then we'll be off."
"Yes, dear."
She went upstairs to change. When she came down, Tom's eyes were on her: "What a picture you look." He took her arm and led her to the car; she felt like royalty.
At the restaurant they ordered their meal and a bottle of champagne, it all went down very well till one of the waiters came up to them and asks them if they had got off alright.

"Yes, thank you. Everything went quite well, they are now on the boat and should be there by tomorrow."
"Give them my regards, will you? We shall miss them, I suppose you will too."
"Yes, we are already and they haven't been gone less than 5 hours."
"Anyway enjoy your meal; by the way the drinks are on the house, as you are one of our regular customers."
"That's very kind of you we will tell them you were asking after them."
"That's alright, enjoy your meal.
"That was unexpected," said Tom. "And nice of them; it just shows you not all people are bad."
"It was a lovely meal. Shall we go for a little walk, down by the river?"
"Why not? It's such a lovely evening, shame to waste it. Let's pay the Bill and be off."
There weren't many people about, just the birds singing, even at this hour. Down by the river they sat and watched the baby ducks and their parents, also the wild rabbits, suddenly a kingfisher flew by.
"Now that's an omen, if I ever saw one."
"What do you mean, dear?"
"Well, it can only mean that luck is on Jane and Ben's side."
"Why, of course, you're properly right."
"We will just have to wait and see, I wished I had brought my camera."
"Never mind, we can do this again sometime, dear. Now I think it's time for home, don't you?"
"OK, you win. I know when I'm beaten."
Arm in arm they walked back home, feeling very happy, at least they still had each other and that's all that mattered. When they got home the phone was ringing.
"I bet that's Jane phoning on the boat, she said she would."
"Well, you had better go and answer it, dear. I will go and put the kettle on, tea or coffee, love?"
"Oh, tea, please. I won't be long."
"Hello, mum; is that you?"
"Yes, dear, it is. Are you alright?"
"Oh, yes, fine, thanks. It's a lovely ship, so smooth, and the food is great. Did you go out for the meal?"
"How did you know about that, dear?"
"We arranged it before we left, we thought you would be a bit upset, and we know you like going out for meals."
"Oh, Jane, you are a wonderful daughter and we love you to bits. That was very thoughtful of you both, thank you. Ring us when you get there, will you?"
"Yes, of course we will; talk to you both soon. Bye for now." Then she hung up. "Is she OK, dear?"
"Yes, they are fine and she sounds very happy."
"That's good then, now we can leave them be and let them get on with their lives."
"I couldn't agree more," said mum.

Tom stayed downstairs for a bit, lit his pipe as he always did when he had something on his mind. *I had better keep an eye on Joyce, I think she will miss them more than she realizes. I will see if some of her friends will help, I'll have a word with them tomorrow.* With that in mind, he too went off to bed.

They both had a good night's sleep. The last two days have been rather hectic; they woke to another sunny day, not quite so hot as the day before. The day started with breakfast and tea on the patio; again the birds were singing, no kingfisher that morning but it was still nice to hear the other birds twittering on.

"What are your plans today, dear?" asked Tom.

"Oh, I think I will do some washing and cleaning, my house has been neglected lately."

"Well, don't overdo it, it's not that bad surely."

"No, but you still need to do it from time to time though, dear."

"Well, I am going into the garden and tend to the roses; they are looking their bests right now."

"I know, I can smell them from the kitchen window."

"I am glad you are enjoying them, I set them for you."

"Yes, I know you did," and she went over to kiss him on the cheek.

"Now, now none of that," he said laughing. "We have work to do."

It was a long morning, they were both busy bees but enjoying themselves.

"Do you want tea or coffee?" asked Joyce.

"Tea, please. Love, let's have it outside again, make use of the weather while it last."

"OK, dear, won't be long."

Just at that moment the phone rang. *Here we go again*, said mum to herself, *I wonder who this can be?* On answering it wasn't long before she recognized the caller.

"Jane," she said. "How wonderful to hear you. How are you both? OK, I hope?"

"Yes, we are fine, we have docked in Bilbao."

"Gosh, you're there already?"

"Yes, we are on our way to our new house, doesn't that sound great? It will seem funny driving on the left. Ben says we will have to get another car; they do that here in Spain. Anyway, this is just a quick call to let you know we arrived over safely."

"Thank you, dear, we will talk again soon."

"Bye for now, mum. Be good, love to dad."

"Who was that, dear?"

"Jane has arrived in Spain, she is OK and sounds really happy."

"That's good to hear. Now where is that tea? I am dry as a bone. "Here we are with some of your favourite biscuits."

Jane and Ben were soon at their new bungalow; it was just as they remember it, there were red and white flowers on the hedges and some geraniums in the front garden. Ben lifted up Jane and carried her over the door step. Jane was full of giggles.

"Come on, Ben, don't be daft; I am dying of thirst now. Let's get the kettle on." "Oh, Jane, isn't it lovely here? I can't believe we are, can you?"

"Well, we are, and there is no turning back now, soon we will get a little dog and then we will be complete. Did you notice the time when we arrived? Only I said I would let mum know what time we got in."
"I think it was about 3 p.m., dear."
Everywhere was looking lovely; they had their tea on the patio they made it a bit special as it was also their anniversary too. Ben had booked a meal for them down by the beach. There were boxes everywhere, Ben said they had all the time in the world to get sorted, but, as usual, Jane couldn't wait. *Women, why do they have to be in such a rush*, said Ben to himself; it didn't bother him if it took months to clear the boxes. By evening most of the work was done; soon it was time to go out for the meal.
It was a lovely warm evening when they got near the sea front, it was buzzing with holiday makers, and they managed to find a shady spot, and went to the restaurant. The air condition was very pleasant and so was the meal. Ben had ordered some champaign as it was a special day for them and it went down a treat. All too soon it was time to go; Ben fancied a walk along the sea front.
"This is what we could do every evening, you know, Jane?" said Ben.
"Yes, dear, we could, we are only 10 minutes away from the sea front."
In fact, from their house they could see the sea. If they looked across the horizon they could just see the mountains.
"We must take some pictures to send back home," said Ben. "I am sure they would love to see the views."
"We could get a laptop, that would be even better," said Jane. "Most people have them nowadays."
"Good idea. We'll have a look at some next week. Shall we make for the car now? It's getting late."
"OK," said Jane. "When we get home I'll phone home, they will be wondering how we are getting on."
It was a lovely drive back; even on a short journey there were some lovely views to look at. They had sorted out the bedroom before they left, so all they had to do was have a nightcap and into bed.
Strangely enough, they both slept well, they woke up to glorious sunshine which they would have to get used to from now on. Ben went to the kitchen; first he found it strange being in a different place, in his own kitchen he knew where things were, so this is another thing he will have to get used to still there's plenty of time.
"Made the tea yet?" Jane shouted to Ben.
"Coming, dear, it took longer than I thought; I couldn't find any of the things I needed."
"Oh, dear," said Jane. "I told you we should have sorted things out yesterday." "Never mind, we will today."
"I knew you would see it my way," said Jane laughing.
"Alright, you win, now let's get breakfast out of the way and then we can start." "My, my, we are bossy this morning. Come on, let's eat. Any more tea, dear?"
"Yes, there is some left in the pot."
"Don't forget we have to drink plenty over here, Ben."

"Yes, I know we do. We will have to take it in turn who makes the tea, or whatever we fancy."
"Shall we get washed up now, then sort out the boxes? Later we could go down to our front for a snack."
"Good idea, Jane, why not?"
They were busy all morning; one of the neighbours came round to say *hola* and to welcome them to the area.

The new neighbours

At around 3 o'clock they were sitting on their neighbours' patio drinking *sangría* and putting the world to rights, when suddenly Ben said to them: "Would you like to come with us tonight for a meal? You can show us the area, and show us the best places to go. I am sure you know lots of them."
"Yes, we do," said John. "We have been out here now for 6 years, so we are getting to know the area pretty well I think."
"Good, then we will see you about 8 p.m. this evening."
Jane and Ben went back home to finish the unpacking; it wasn't long before everything was shipshape. Ben went onto the patio, he lit his pipe and drank his beer; he was a very happy man, now he could enjoy his life, what more could he want? A lovely wife and home, this is what he worked for, and now he was going to enjoy every second of it. Jane was in the bedroom, getting ready for the evening out with their first new found friends, they were a lovely couple about the same age as her and Ben and shared the same interest as them, so they were well suited. Shirley told Jane that people out here go in for barbeques so they suggested that they tried one at the weekend.
"Good idea," the men said. "We will get the meat organized tomorrow, and Ben can get the drinks, it will be a welcome party. Once you get the hang of barbequing there will be no stopping you. You see if I am right."
"Well you two, are you ready to paint the town red?"
"My, Jane, you do look nice," said John. Shirley had to agree. Ben couldn't take his eyes of her either; he has never seen his wife looking so happy in ages.
"Well, now, John, are we going in your car?"
"Of course as I know the way so jump in all of you and let's go, I am getting rather hungry."
"So am I," said Ben.
It was a good drive to the restaurant, any further and the girls would have been asleep. The car came to a sudden halt which brought the girls back to life, at last.
Jane said: "We are here. Oh, what a charming place! It's wonderful, and look at the parakeets!" Squeals of delight came from Jane's lips, the men laughed at her. It didn't bother Shirley too much as she was used to them; it was a picture to see Jane's face light up.

“Well, come on, let’s find a table and eat, drink and be merry.” said John.
They ordered two bottles of wine and asked for a steak well done. It was absolutely delicious, and the atmosphere was electric. They enjoyed themselves so much that they hadn’t realized what the time was.
“Goodness, is that the time? Would you like a nightcap at our place?” said Ben.
“I wouldn’t mind,” said John. How about you, dear?”
“Yes, fine by me. Let’s pay the Bill and make for home.
Soon they were sitting down in Jane’s kitchen. The men went outside for a smoke; Ben got out his pipe.
“Oh, you smoke a pipe then, Ben? I myself never took to one.”
“I have always smoked one, but Jane doesn’t like me having one in the house, she says it’s a bad habit and I should give it up, but I really enjoy it.”
“Well, then if you enjoy it, why not?”
The girls were having a girlie chat.
“Hark at those two, it sounds as though they have been friends for years, not just a few days.”
“I am glad they have got on well, Jane won’t be lonely now. Were OK too, are we not?”
“Yes, of course we are, it would be great if we go out together, wouldn’t it?”
“Yes, I think it would.”
“Well, Shirley, are you ready for home? I think we have kept these good people up rather late. We have had a lovely evening, must do it again soon.”
“Good night, see you soon.”
Outside the air still felt warm, the sky was clear: you could read a newspaper in the twilight.
“Did you enjoy the evening, Shirley?” said John. “They are nice people.”
“Yes, they are. I am sure we will become good friends in no time. Now I am going to bed, coming, dear?”
“Won’t be long, love, just got to lock up.”
They had a good lie in, longer then they should have done, but what did it matter? They had all the time in the world. Ben was in the kitchen when Jane got up.
“Oh, I was just going to bring you a cup of tea” said Ben.
“Thank you, dear, that’s kind of you. My turn tomorrow then.”
“What are we going to do today?”
“Well, I thought we could try that beach near San Pedro; they have some lovely shops there as well, so Shirley said.”
“Oh, that’s what you were talking about last night.”
“Yes, she was telling me a few things about our area. One day she said she would show me. I like her, we get on fine.”
“I am pleased you do. John and I get on OK too.”
“So we have made our first friends already. Now then everything has been put away so we can enjoy ourselves.”
“What about breakfast?”
“I think I will just have toast and jam,” said Jane.

"Well, I am having bacon and egg, and coffee."
"OK, dear, it won't be long, are we having it outside?"
"Why not? It's a beautiful day again; I suppose it will always be like this."
"Well, it is a hot country after all," said Jane laughing.
Soon they were outside having their breakfast, and the birds were in good voice again.
"Isn't it lovely to hear the birds and the parrots?" Just then the squirrels came into the garden.
"Oh, look, see that baby one. She has some nuts in her mouth."
Ben laughed: "They're not nuts, dear, but dates of our tree. Look, there she goes."
"Oh, are they sweet?"
"Yes, they are, but they had better stay outside, otherwise they will make a mess everywhere. John warned me about them last night, also the cats are a bit of a problem too, and they shouldn't be encouraged."
"But surely a dog wouldn't hurt, would it?"
"No, a dog's fine as long as it's on a lead."
"That's good then," said Jane. "That's what we will get."
"Soon, dear, in a few months maybe, when we are more settled."
"OK, I'll wait a while longer but not too long, mind."
"We'll see" said Ben and went away for his pipe smiling to himself.
As he walked away, Jane looked at him and thought: *He has some thing on his mind and he is not telling me, but I will find out soon enough; see if I don't, Mr. Smarty Pants.* She went off to do the washing up; by mid morning the work was finished. She took some coffee outside to Ben, he was talking to John.
"Hello," said John. "What have you been up to?"
"Oh, just the washing up and a bit of tiding up. It's a lovely day," said Jane. "We are going down to the beach later; it will be cooler near the sea."
"Yes, it will be" said John.
When Jane came out to see Ben, they were talking quietly. *I am sure they are up to something*, thought Jane to herself, *I wonder what they are cooking up, something's happening, I am sure of it.*
She went back inside to get ready for the beach.
"Are you ready, Ben? It's about 3 p.m."
"OK, dear, I will be with you in a minute."
When they arrived at the beach, it was packed; lucky they found a shady parking space. They got as near to the sea as they could. Jane brought her book and Ben just relaxed in his chair, soon fell asleep. Jane was enjoying her book but her eyelids refused to stay open. When they both woke up, they were very thirsty and decided to go for a drink at one of the bars nearby. "Goodness, it's tea time already." It certainly was cooler near the sea.
It was late when they arrived home. They had one more nightcap and went off to bed; they slept quite well, but it was a very humid night and Jane did a lot of tossing and turning, so Ben made her lie in a bit longer. He went into the kitchen and made some toast and coffee, soon Jane came thorough, blur eyed.

"Hello, love, you OK this morning?"
"No, not really. I must have had too much sun yesterday; I feel a bit off-colour. I really don't want any breakfast, just a drink, would you make me one?"
"Of course, darling, you go back to bed. I will put the air con on for you."
"Thank you, dear, you're most kind."
Jane went back to bed, Ben was getting a bit worried about her: "It's not like Jane to give in so easily. I am just going next door, Jane, won't be long."
"Hello, Ben," said John. "What is the matter? You're looking worried."
"It's Jane; she doesn't look too good this morning. Do you think Shirley could come round and see her? I think she might be a bit dehydrated."
When Shirley went round she found Jane in the bathroom.
"Goodness me," she cried. "You really are off colour! I think we ought to take you down to the local hospital to get you checked over."
For once in Jane's life, she never objected: she felt too poorly.
Ben came back, and already Jane and Shirley were on their way; Ben got the car keys and drove them there. It was a short drive and soon Jane was getting sorted out, there was a blood test to have and blood pressure was taken. Jane was admitted that same day under observation: blood test shown she was suffering from some kind of food poisoning and dehydration. The doctors wanted to know where they had eaten as they had to do a check on the restaurant. Ben went back home to get some things for Jane, by this time they put her onto a drip and she was told to drink lots of water; food was out of the question, anyway she never felt like eating, it made her feel so weak. Shirley and John came to see her in the afternoon, Ben was coming in later. Ben gave the things to Shirley to give to Jane. Most of the time, she just slept, and only woke when the nurses came to her, drink was important: the sooner she took more fluids she would feel a lot better.
The doctors told Ben that in 48 hours she should be OK. They made contact with the restaurant and it was closed down for a week, as a few more people were brought in. The nurses were wonderful to Jane and the doctors were too. John and Ben had a wonderful surprise waiting for Jane when she came home, late that afternoon. Shirley knew about it but she was sworn to secrecy, it was Jane's birthday in a few days time, but as this happened then it seemed a good time, it would certainly cheer her up. Shirley went to collect Jane from the hospital while John and Ben went to collect the puppy. It was a golden Labrador only 8 weeks old, very cute. On the way home they called in at the pet shop to get a basket and a lead and a few toys, also, of course, some dog food.
When they arrived home Jane and Shirley were in the garden.
"Oh, here come Ben and John, they have a smile from ear to ear," said Jane. "I wonder what they have been up too. Hello, you two! What have you been up to this afternoon?"
"We have a surprise for you, Jane, come and see."
"What on earth could it be? It's not my birthday till next week."
"As you have been poorly, we thought you can have it now."
"Oh, Ben, you're so good to me! You are always thinking about me."

"You are a very lucky girl," said John. "Anyway, come and see what you have got.
"Oh, Ben, isn't he the most adorable puppy I have ever seen? Is he really mine?"
"Yes, dear, all yours. We hope you both become firm friends."
"Oh, I am sure we will."
"Right; then let's take him into the garden and show him his new home."
"Oh, look Shirley, he wants to play with his ball. Isn't he sweet? You and I can share him."
"What about me?!" said Ben, laughing.
"Oh, of course you as well, well, all of us really. What food did you get him?"
"Well, the man at the pet shop said he was to have puppy food for the next few weeks, and then we shall have to start training him soon."
"I can see we will not get any work done now, what have I done!"
"Yes, we will, dear, we can do it while he is asleep."
"There is no sign of him doing that yet, he is full of energy."
"Coming home," said John. "I am getting hungry. We will come back later to see how things are going."
Ben went off to start on dinner; all the drama of the last few days forgotten. At least that had done the trick, he had never seen Jane so happy; she was like a child again.
Jane came into the kitchen: "Oh, look, he is following me."
"Right," said Ben. "Now tell him to sit and stay.
The puppy looked at Jane, then at Ben: "Sit," said Jane.
"That's good. Your basket is over there, young man."
"Do you think he will answer you?" said Jane laughing.
"Well, no: he has to know who is the boss from the start."
"Yes, of course he has. Shall we let him into the lounge?"
"OK, dear. I will just finish dinner."
"It smells good," said Jane. "Oh, Ben, dear, look!"
"Now what is he doing?"
"He is trying to jump onto the chair."
"Well, don't encourage him to do that; his basket is over there, put him in it and come and get your dinner."
When Jane turned round he was fast asleep, he did look cute.
"We had better phone mum and dad and tell her about the happenings of the last few days. Thank you for the dinner, it was lovely."
Jane was on the phone for quite a while; she sounded very happy. Ben went to get his pipe and took the tea outside. It was turning out to be a very happy day after all. The puppy was settling in nicely, he woke up and Ben started playing with him.
"I think we are going to get on just fine, won't we, son?"
"WHOOF!"
Ben laughed: "Hear that, Jane? He just barked at me!!"
"Silly, that's what dogs do!" said Jane. "Now where is my tea?"
"We shall have to find a name for him," Ben said. "Can you think of one?"
"How about Bouncer?"
"Yes, that suits him; he is always bouncing around, isn't he?"

"Well, yes he is, but he will soon grow out of it."
In the afternoon they tried putting a collar and lead on him, but all he wanted to do was chew on it, so after a few more tries they gave in.
"We will try again later; he has got to get used to it though," said Ben. "Otherwise we won't be able to take him for a walk."
"He may be better next time" said Jane.
"We'll see," with that, he hunged it up in the kitchen. The dog followed and looked at Ben. "Yes, you naughty dog, you are going to have it on one day, see if you don't."
"Woof." Bouncer said, and went to find Jane.
"What is the matter, Bouncer? What have you been up to?" He rolled over and wanted Jane to play with him; the little dog went into the garden playing with his ball, then he found some leaves rustling in the wind. "You are playful today. Good, when you're asleep I can get some work done." Sure enough there he was asleep in his bed, looking as though butter wouldn't melt in his mouth.

Training days begin for Bouncer!!!

July was to be a very busy month for Ben and Jane, the training sessions for Bouncer began in earnest. Their training adviser came three times a week, as they both wanted to teach him properly. Bouncer liked his new trainer, he offered him tit bits when he did it right, so of course Bouncer soon learnt when he was onto a good thing. Golden Labradors are well known to be good dogs to work with, they respond to kindness so it didn't take him long to learn new tricks. Shirley and John came to watch them play.
"That was very good," said John. "He's soon learnt how to do that, hasn't he?"
"Yes, and that's not all he has learnt," said Ben proudly. "Just you watch this, this is what his trainer taught him the other day." Ben went too threw the ball and Bouncer caught it and brought it straight back to him. "Good boy," said Ben. "Here is your treat."
"That was very good," said Shirley. "What his he like on his lead now?"
"Very good now," said Ben. "He didn't like it at first, but now he goes and finds it himself."
"Good, then can we take him for a walk tomorrow down by the lake?"
"Of course you can. In fact, I was going to ask you if you would have him for the morning. We have some business to see to in town and we daren't leave him at home yet on his own."
"We would love to have him, wouldn't we, John?"
"No problem" said John.
So it was settled Shirley was to fetch him in the morning. The training session he was having made him tired so he slept a lot more in his basket. Now Jane could get on with some housework while Ben did some gardening, although there

wasn't much to do, not like the one back home. He said as much to Jane the other day: "I think I will get myself an allotment, just a small one to keep me busy."
"Good idea," said Jane.
"I think we go to the town hall for that," said Ben "We could always try."
Ben got the car out and soon they were at the solicitors.
"Good morning," he said speaking very good English.
"Your English is very good," said Jane. "Where did you learn that?"
"I went to a school in London and then I got a job over here."
"Thank goodness you did, you have saved us a fortune."
"Well, now what can I do for you, good people?"
"My name is Mr. Ben Johnson and this is my wife. We have come here today to sort out our will; we have a few shares in certain places."
"That is not a problem Mr Johnson I can certainly do that for you."
"Good" said Ben, who was doing all the talking. Jane just sat there listening.
Ben seems to know what he his talking about, thought Jane. It all seemed to come to an end quickly. They paid him and he said he would be in touch shortly.
"Right," said Ben. "Let's go and eat and have a coffee, shall we, dear?"
"Yes, why not? We haven't got to be back until 3. They sat at a table near the beach, it was a lovely sunny day, not a cloud in the sky, they had a salmon salad for their lunch and a cool drink. Ben had a beer.
"I feel a lot happier now that's sorted" said Ben.
"Good!" said Jane. "Now you can tell me all about it, because I didn't understand what was going on."
"Well, shall we discuss this back home? It's nothing really to worried about, love."
"Yes, alright then, I will wait till I get home, soon it will all be revealed. You know what, Ben? I think I will go for a swim later, do you want to come too?"
"I might, love, I will see."
When they arrived home, John came to meet them at the gate.
"Everything OK, John?"
"Yes, of course. Did it all go well for you?"
"Yes, it did, John. Now we can start putting our other plans into action."
"What plans are them then, old chap?"
"Well, if it's OK by you, can I pop round this evening, and I will tell you all about it?"
"Tell you what, do you fancy a beer down at our local? You haven't been there yet, have you?"
"No, I haven't," said Ben. "What a good idea! Shall we say about 8.30? Fine then John, see you then".
Ben went back home only to find Bouncer and Jane fast asleep; he was lying on her knee.
"It didn't take you long to find a comfy place, did it, young man?"
"Woof" said Bouncer as soon as Ben walked in, with that, Jane woke up.
"Why don't you go and lie down on the bed for a bit, dear?"

"I think I will, darling" she said.
"Oh, by the way, John and I are going for a drink at John's local tonight, love; you don't mind do you?"
"Of course not, you go and enjoy yourself. Shirley and I are going shopping one day next week, I want some more things for our home."
"Oh, good," said Ben. "Then I shan't feel so guilty shall I?"
With that, Jane went for her nap. Bouncer stayed in his basket.
All was quite in the Johnson's household, only the birds were singing. Ben took out his pipe and had a quite read of his paper. After a while Ben looked at the clock.
"Goodness me, is that the time already?! I had better start getting dinner ready. I'll leave Jane a bit longer, she looks so peaceful."
He set the table, put out the glasses for the wine; he had made a lovely salad, one of Jane's favourites, and left the bread and butter till last. He stood back and gave a sigh of relief. *There, it looks good enough for a queen, I think*. Soon he heard footsteps coming through the dining room, he turn round and saw Bouncer looking at him first, then at his bowl.
"What's up, Bouncer, do you want some dinner too? You are a cleaver dog. OK, you win, I will get some for you and some water. "Good boy we will play out side for a bit as not to wake Jane."
"Woof, woof!"
"Shoos, there's a good dog, otherwise you will wake her, then she will get cross with both of us, won't she?"
"Woof!"
"Come on, let's get you outside, you noisy thing." Outside the air was very warm and humid. "Goodness me," said Ben. There isn't a breeze anywhere today! I'll just go and sort out the air conditioner, that should do the trick."
"Woof, woof!"
"Be quite now, Bouncer, you are being noisy this afternoon, bad dog."
Bouncer laid down sulking and went to sleep.

Preparations under way for the long awaited trip

Ben went round to see John that same evening. It wasn't far to John's local so they could have a few drinks. "Hello, Ben, come in, it will be a moment, just putting on my shirt, then we will go. It's such a lovely evening, isn't it? We will bring the girls down here one night, it will make a change for them. How are you settling in?"
"OK, thanks, John."
"Well now what's this all about? You're not thinking of going back to the UK, are you?"
"No, it's nothing like that, a few years ago Jane and I were planning to do a bit of cruising, but never real found the time until now, so we are thinking of doing it soon."

“So what’s the problem than?”
“Well, other than having Bouncer none. We were wondering if you would have him for two months.”
“Of course we will, he his used to us now and doing well with his training, which of course we shall keep up for you, Ben.”
“Well, thanks very much; it will be a load off our minds knowing he is in good hands. We will let you know when we have sorted out everything, bye for now.”
When Ben arrived home, Jane was on the phone to her sister Jean, who had just come back from Cyprus. Like Jane’s dad she had a cancer scare too; she was given the all clear a week ago, but she has to go for blood tests just like her dad. When Jane came over to Spain she was away on holiday, so missed out on all the family fun. Jane was telling her about their next adventure and if Bill and she would like to join them.
“I would love to, but I shall have to go and ask him, he his just having a cuppa.”
She came back sounding very excited at the idea: “We shall have to sort out which port to go from. You will have to meet us where ever we are, Jean.”
“Of course we will, that’s no problem. Oh, it’s been a lovely year so far, what with you moving to Spain, now we are going on an adventure… You were always a wild one, always doing something different.”
“Yes, that’s right, I suppose I was, Jean. Well, now I must go take Bouncer for his walk.”
“Oh, yes, I heard you got a dog now. How’s he doing with his training?
“Very well indeed, he loves getting his treats, so he does well so he can get them.”
“He’s a cleaver dog then?”
“He likes to go down to the pond in the park where the ducks are and a few squirrels.”
“It all sounds lovely you are lucky, Jane, wish I was over there with you.”
“Well, what’s stopping you doing that? Once your house is sold it’s plain sailing, as they say.”
“We will have to think about it when we come back from our adventure. Anyway, I must go now to sort out dinner, talk to you all later.”
Ben came into the kitchen. Jane was having coffee.
“I’ve just put the kettle on, do you want some coffee?”
“Yes, please, love. I have just been talking to John about our forthcoming adventure.”
“What did he say? Was he surprised?”
“Yes, he was. He thought we were settled here now we have the dog. He didn’t know that we were going to do it before we came here, but as we sold earlier than expected no, but now the time is right: it’s now or never, am I right, Jane, love?”
“Yes, of course you are. I have asked Jean and they would like to come with us.”
“Well, later on we will get the maps out and have a good look, we will have to decide how long we will be away. When are Bill and Jean starting their new jobs?”
“I don’t know, I forgot to ask them that. Once we know where and when we are going I’ll phone them. I am getting excited thinking about it, are you?”

"Yes, but it's going to be hard work, learning how to handle a boat, specially on the Med., we will have to make sure we do it properly, for our own safety."
"Aye, aye, captain!"
"Yes, that's another thing we will have to decide: who will be in charge? We can't have too many bossy."
"Bill can't boss anyone around, he's as gentle as a lamb" said Jane.
"Yes, maybe he his, but it might do him good.
"Anyway, let's get dinner over, and get the maps out shall we?"
The dinner was soon over and washed down with wine and coffee. They took the maps out to the patio. John saw them and Jane invited him over.
"What have we here then?" he said.
"Just a few maps to get us going," said Ben. "Have you any ideas?"
"Well, how about the Canary islands? Do they have birds on them then?" said Jane.
"I should think so somewhere" and they both laughed.
"It doesn't sound a bad idea," said Ben. "Let's have another look."
"Who fancies another drink? All this hard work's making me thirsty."
"You call this hard?" said Ben. "Wait until we get on that boat, you will soon see what hard work is."
"Yes," John said. "I'll vouch for that, I once did some sailing myself and although it was fun it was jolly hard work, but enjoyable."
With that Jane went to get the drinks; she found some ice cubs, put them into the orange and sliced a piece of orange at the side of the glass, just like they do in the restaurants.
"They look nice," said John. "Can't wait to taste them."
Half an hour and it was all sorted.
"Thanks to John, he seems to know his way around the world. We forgot about him being in the Navy, he should be coming with us" said Ben, but unfittingly it was the wrong time of the year for him.
"Whose turn is it to take Bouncer for his evening walk?'
"If you don't mind, could Shirley and I take him? We haven't had much to do with him lately, and as we are going to have him for a while soon, it would help us to get to know him better, don't you think?"
"A good idea," said Ben. "I'll just go and get him for you. Here boy, where are you? Time for a walk with John."
"Woof!" said Bouncer.
"I would if that means a yes. Bouncer does love his walk, he his getting very good on his lead now, in fact he fetches it for us."
"It might be a good idea if he stayed over one or to nights to see how he gets on?"
"Yes, I think so, we shall have to arrange it soon."
With that they all went off for their walk, with Bouncer wagging his tail and barking with excitement.
Ben and Jane went back inside to do some more map reading, they found it would be nearer to go to Cartagena for their start of the journey, the next day they would make some enquires about hiring a boat of some kind.

They were late in bed that night. Jane said she was too excited to sleep, and Ben was still doing some research. This is when he could have done with Bill's knowledge, as he was also a Navy man just like John was. Ben was in the RAF, he was a fighter pilot. Ben took his pipe outside with his nightcap, and sat there for some time, when a voice appeared from nowhere. "Goodness, you startled me, John!"

"I've just brought Bouncer back, he has been good as gold. He is such a lovely dog, we are thinking of getting one now."

"Oh, good for you both. They are such good company aren't they?"

"Yes, they are. How are the preparations going, any progress?"

"Oh, yes, we are going to start our journey from Cartagena. Tomorrow we are contacting someone from the harbour, then it's just finding the time to go. Once we have sorted out our shipping transport and times of travel, etc., and all our paper work that's needed then we are ready for the off."

"Good for you, Ben. I bet Jane is getting excited."

"Any thing new she always is, we think she should have been a gipsy: always wants to go off somewhere; one day she will settle down. Well, mate, thanks for taking him. We will have to arrange when he is coming to stay."

"Yes, OK, I'll leave it with you, Ben. See you soon, bye, Bouncer!"

"Woof!" said Bouncer. He ran indoors to find Jane, only to find she had gone to bed. He knew he wasn't allowed in the bedroom, so he went in the kitchen to find some water and food. *Boy, that walk was good. Makes me hungry and thirsty; if I get walks like that every day when I stay with them, it will be OK*, thought Bouncer, then barked more to himself than anybody, he went in search of his basket and went to sleep.

Ben came in and saw Bouncer: "Goodness me, you must have had a good walk. I've no worries about them taking care of you boy."

Ben made sure everywhere was locked up, and then went off to bed; he was very tired after all the book work, but it will be worth it, tomorrow will take care of itself. Soon he too was fast asleep. Jane was up first and made Ben a cup of tea; he was still fast asleep so she just left it at his bed side. She went back downstairs to make some toast, suddenly Bouncer came running in.

"Steady boy, you will knock things over."

"Woof, woof!"

"Shush, you will wake Ben, let him sleep in a bit longer. What's up? Do you want to go into the garden?"

"Woof" he said again, and as soon as Jane opened the door he was off like a shot. He found his ball and brought it into the kitchen.

"No, no, Bouncer, not in here. When I have had my breakfast, I shan't be long."

With that he went back outside again, laid under his favourite tree. He started chewing his bone; he did that when he was bored. He couldn't wait till Ben woke up; he always played with him, and gave him titbits whereas Jane didn't; only when he has worked for them, then she will.

It was such a lovely hot day Bouncer decided to go and find some rabbits to chase just for fun. In the garden there was a huge tree, behind it was a stream; he knew he wasn't suppose to go there, but he was in a very playful mood that day and he didn't

really care where he went. Anyway his owners were to busy to worry about him and John and Shirley weren't nowhere around, so he thought he would entertain himself for a while, in other words, being a naughty dog.
Bouncer managed somehow to get behind the tree near the stream; he saw a rabbit and chased after it. Of course it ran faster than him, not realising how far he had gone, when he looked back the house was no longer in sight, and the further away from the house he went the more lost he got. There was a pool of water, he drank it but as it was a warm day and it didn't taste quite the same back home, but suddenly he recognized something. Of course! The park John and Shirley took him there the other day. He ran towards the pond, barked at the ducks and chased a squirrel; he ran under a tree, laid down and went to sleep.
Meanwhile, back home unaware of Bouncer's antics, Ben was having his breakfast not knowing anything about Bouncer's disappearance and carried on with his breakfast.
All of a sudden Ben shouted to Jane: "Bouncer's quiet isn't he, Jane?"
"Yes, he is. I better go and check on him. He was a bit cross with me earlier 'cause I would not play with him.
"Bouncer, here, boy, where are you?!" Ben looked all round the garden to no avail.
"He's not in the garden, Jane, I wonder where he his."
"Have you checked John's? You know he likes it there."
"Good idea! I'll try that."
"Have you seen Bouncer, John?"
"No," he said. "Not since yesterday. Why, what's up, Ben?"
"He's gone missing a good hour or so; we thought he was in the garden."
"Hang on, I'll get the car out; he couldn't have gone far. Don't worry, we'll soon have him back."
They told Jane where they were going and set off; they took their mobiles with them just in case he returned home. They rode along the stream where Bouncer went chasing the rabbit, then he spotted the park and he knew where he was; but Ben and John didn't know, until they saw some people laughing and shouting.
"Hello, what's going on here?" said Ben. "Oh, look, there he is chasing that duck, he thinks it's a game, poor thing! Let's rescue it, John. Bouncer come here boy! You bad dog, you don't go chasing ducks."
Bouncer went down on all fours, tail between his legs. He knew he was in trouble, but just the same he enjoyed his morning, it was worth it.
"We will have to find out how he got out of the garden."
When Ben put Bouncer in his basket, he went out in the garden to find out where he was getting out.
"Oh, I see, the little monkey, that's where he got out. Right, I'll soon fix that, see if I don't."
It didn't take long it was all sorted. Putting his tools away, Ben went back into the kitchen ignoring Bouncer, who was pretending to be asleep.
"Yes, you naughty dog, I know you are looking at me with one eye open. You will not escape easily next time."
Jane came in to start dinner: "Goodness, he does look sorry for himself."
"Now don't go all soft on him, Jane, he's got to learn he can't have all his own way."

"I know, dear, I think he is sorry now though. It will soon be his supper time, or his he band from that as well?"
"No, don't be silly, I just wanted to make sure he understands, that's all."
"I'm sure he does, come on, Bouncer, dinner time."
"Woof" he barked, tail now wagging. "Woof," he went up to Ben and licked him all over.
"Alright, I know I'm linked. Bouncer, that's enough." Ben and Jane started to laugh.
"You couldn't stay mad at Bouncer for long, soon he will be staying with John, and we don't think that's going to go down well with him."
Later on Ben took him for his afternoon walk, which he loved, he ran down the garden as though he hadn't be out for ages, which was not true, as it was only a few hours ago when he escaped, but never again. It was a lovely warm evening; Ben decided to go for a pint at his local. While he was there John came in.
"Hello," he said. "Fancied a quite tipple."
"Can't blame you, it's a lovely cool night. What's Jane doing?"
"Oh, she's washing up, then she giving her mum a ring telling her about our forthcoming trip."
"Oh, of course; not long now, is it? Have you got it sorted?"
"Oh, yes, almost there, John, just the last few hitches."
"Wish I was coming with you."
"Maybe next time."
"I am looking forward in taking charge of Bouncer."
On hearing his name, he looked up and saw it was John; he liked him, he always gave him titbits and now it was no exception.
"He knows what he's looking for, doesn't he?" He had his nose in John's pocket.
"Alright, alright," said John. Here you are, no there's no more left. Has he got over his antics?"
"Think so," said Ben. "He can't get out no more, it's all be blocked off."
"That's good then," said John. "Well, Bouncer, old boy, see you soon; be good."
"Woof, woof!" said Bouncer, as though he understood every word.
"Come on then, we better go too."
They both walked home together.

Preparing for the trip

A few weeks later Bouncer was sent off to the Jackson's for his long stay; they took his bed and toys just as you would do for a child, to make him feel at home. Although he knew them quite well it was good to have your own things around you.
Jane heard from Jean and Bill they were making their way to the port, staying in the hotel nearby. It was a lovely hotel overlooking the harbour, there were lots of boats of all shapes and sizes.
"I wonder which one will be ours" said Jean.

"I don't think it's in yet," said Bill. "It should be in on Friday, so Ben said."
"I can't wait to see them again, it's been ages."
"I know love, but it won't be long now, time will soon pass. Now let's go and see what's for dinner, I'm starving."
Ben made contact with Bill the following Friday, to know if they would be able to book another room at their hotel, as the boat won't be in while Monday morning, around 10 a.m.
"Sure, Ben, I'll see what I can do, and I'll ring you back. How's Jane?"
"Looking forward to the trip, she can't wait to see you both."
"Has Bouncer settled in with John? He sounds a nice chap."
"Oh, he his, he loves Bouncer as much as we do."
"Oh, that's good then. OK, Ben, I'll give you a ring soon, bye for now."
It was late evening when Bill called back: "I've booked you in at the hotel for Friday, looking forward in seeing you, bye for now."
It was all go at the Johnson's household, lots of phone calls were made. Jane's mum was quite surprised that they were going away so soon, after all they hadn't been in Spain long. Surely the trip could have waited a bit longer, said mum and dad had to agree. Anyway they wished them *bon voyage* and safe passage. The following day they made their way down to Cartagena. It was a long drive, they stopped for a snack at one of the bars, brought some more water and carried on with their journey. At around 6 p.m. they arrived at the hotel, Jean and Bill were outside to greet them.
"Well, well, look what the cats brought in?"
"That's a nice greeting I must say. How are you both?"
"Oh, we're fine, can't wait to get this show on the road."
"We feel the same, don't we, Jane?" said Ben.
"Anyway come inside and we'll show you your room."
"It looks a lovely hotel, where did you find it?"
"Oh, on the Internet it was so simple to book."
"That's where we found our boat, they were ever so helpful, weren't they, Ben?"
"Yes, they were. They gave us some maps of the area we want to visit and lots of more information, about an hour and it was all sorted."
"Well, the room's fine," they said. "We will discuss the program later shall we?"
"Is there any gardens around here?" said Jane.
"Yes," said Jean. "Look, I'll show you."
Once outside the view was magnificent: "What a good photo this would take to show mum back home!"
Jean and Jane went back on the patio and ordered drinks.
"I wonder where the boys have gone" said Jane.
"Oh, I think they went for a tour round the hotel and to discuss the trip."
"Ben's getting quite excited about it."
"Oh, yes, so is Bill, there like two peas in a pod as they say" and they both laughed.
About an hour went by, and they caught up with the girls.
"There you are," they said. "Have you had a good look round, and does it meet with your approval?"

"Oh, yes, it's a lovely setting and the gardens are beautiful."
"Did you see the peacock and the squirrels, Jane?"
"Yes, I did. They are lovely, I took some photos to show mum."
"Good," said Ben. "Let's go and eat, I'm starving."
"So are we," said the girls. "Come on then."
They found the dining room, the air con was very welcoming, they found their table and sat down to eat. The waiter came and took their order, they had bubbly and steak, medium rare for Jane; steak was her favourite with onion rings and chunky chips, what more could a girl ask for! All too soon the meal came to an end, washed down with a coffee. They all retired to the lounge to discuss the forthcoming adventure; at this point they were all getting excited.
"Slow down all of you, we can't talk all at once!"
It was about 11 when they returned to their adjoining rooms. Ben said he needed a nightcap, found some brandy in his room. Jane had a shady. Soon they were fast asleep, they were so tired after their long journey, but unknown to them things were going to be a lot tougher than they thought.
When they awoke, bright sunshine filled the room.
"It's going to be another hot day" said Ben to Jane, who was just waking up. "What time is it?" he asked her.
"About 8, I think, time for breakfast."
They got themselves dressed and went down to the dining room. There was quite a few people there already, still no sign of Bill and Jean.
"Must be having a lie in," said Jane. "Oh, no, here they are."
"Morning you two, did you sleep well?"
"We had a good sleep, thanks; our air con is wonderful, did you?"
"Yes, we were so tired from our journey, it did not take us that long to get off."
"Now then what's for breakfast? Just help yourself, Ben, over there."
"OK, thanks!!"
They found a table by the window looking out to the sea.
"What a lovely view!" said Ben, and Jane had to agree.
"When do we set sail?" said Jean.
"Oh, not until Monday; then it depends on the shipping forecast, doesn't it?" said Bill.
"Yes it does, I've checked it out earlier and I think it will be OK though."
"Oh, good, I can not wait to get started."
"What's the boat called?" asked Bill.
"Oh, didn't I tell you? It's called *The Little Mermaid*, what do you think of that?"
"That's cool," said Jane. "Let's hope she's a good sailor. Just one of my little jokes.
"Well, they can't get no worse than that" laughed Ben.
After breakfast they all decided to go for a walk along the sea front; there was quite a bit of breeze coming of the sea, there were couples holding hands and some with their dogs, children building sand castles... The sea was quite calm, as Ben and Jane looked across the horizon there was a boat coming in.
"Look, isn't that our boat coming in?"

"It's early if it is, let's go and look."
They ran to the edge of the sea.
"I believe you're right, love."
"Yes, it is. Can you see the boat?" Bill shouted to Ben.
"Look there she is! That's the one we are going to work on. "
"Goodness me, big, isn't it? Think we can handle a boat that size?
"A bit to late now to have second thoughts, eh Bill?
"Let's go down to the harbour and see it come in."
"Good idea" said Jane, and off they went. As they neared the harbour their boat was just coming in.
"Doesn't it look lovely?, and look there's a name on its side; yes it says *Mermaid.* What lovely colours they've painted her! Green, red, yellow and blue for the sea. Can we go and have a look inside?"
"Let's go and ask that man over there."
"Now then, ladies, what can I do for ye?"
Talking in a funny accent, Ben said: "Em, can we have a look inside, mate, wè hope to take it out on Monday morning."
"Who ´e´ you might be then? You're not Mr, Johnson, are you?"
"Well, as a matter of fact I am."
"Well, in that case do come on board; it is sure a lovely boat. Have ye got a skipper mate?, cause if ye haven't I'll sure like to sail her for ye."
"Well, my good friend here was in the navy some years ago, so I'm sure we'll be OK, maybe next time."
"Ye that's what they all say. You take care of it and yourselves. See ye when ye get back."
"You never gave me your name."
"Aye, it's Jim you'll be talking to, don't forget it. I'll be keeping my ears open for ye on the shipping channel, that's if you know how to use one." With that he went on his way chuckling to himself.
"He thinks were a joke," said Ben. "We'll show him, won't we, everyone?"
"Yes, we'll show him" they all said together and went down below.
"Look at this," the girls said. "Isn't it cosy? Everything you need, can't wait till Monday.
On Sunday they had a quite day relaxing by the sea; it was a lot cooler down there, and they were talking non-stop about their adventure. In the evening they had their last meal in their favourite restaurant, plenty of wine and some Spanish music thrown in for good measure. They were really letting their hair down. Why not? Little did they know what lay ahead of them, there were many surprises waiting for them. The following morning every one was up and about, they had a big breakfast and soon it was time to go down to the harbour. The sun was out, there was a bit of a breeze but never the less it felt quite pleasant. Once on the boat there was no turning back, this was what they had been waiting for so long and everyone was getting quite excited. Jane especially, she couldn't contain herself. They were really going to have that adventure after all, and they were looking forward tomorrow. All

of them went to bed early; they were packed and ready to go, they had a good night's sleep, but Jane was so excited that it took her a while to drop off and when she finely got off it was time to get up, however it was such a lovely morning and it was going to be a very exciting day. When she got down to the lounge they were all waiting for her.

"What's up?" she asked. "Have I missed something?"

"Have you forgotten what day it is today?"

"No, I don't think so, I know were going on an adventure if that's what you mean."

"Yes, that's right, we are."

"So what then?"

"Well, it's mum and dad's golden wedding and we won't be there to celebrate it with them."

"Oh, dear, of course. Well, we shall have to get on the Internet and see if we can send flowers and a card, and when we get back we can do something then."

"Yes, that would be a good idea," said Ben. "Now can we all go and get some breakfast? I'm starving."

After breakfast they gathered their things together, and went to pay their bill. Everyone came out side to see them off, *safe journey* they all shouted. It was only a short drive to the harbour and it wasn't long before they saw their boat. It was absolutely gleaming, it was a lovely sight to see, they arrived at the jetty; the man who bought the boat in was waiting for them.

"Well, I'll be look who we have here, the captain himself."

"Are you all ready for the off then, sir? Wish I was coming with ye."

"There he goes talking in that funny accent again. It's no good, I've got to find out where he's from," being the inquisitive type, it was Jane who approached him. Walking up to him: "Can I ask you where you're from?"

"Aye, you can, why do you ask? Can't you guess?"

"Noo! I would like to know."

"Well, I am from the Scottish island. I am a true Scott."

"Do you play the mag pipes? And wear a kilt?"

"Aye, that I do. Any more questions, my lady? I've to be on my way. Good luck to you all and take care of The Mermaid, do ye hear?" With that he was on his way.

While the girls were chatting the boys were getting familiarized with the boat; it was well built and very compact, below deck there was a small kitchen, a small toilet and a shower, four beds which folded away, leaving room for table and seats at the side.

"Come on, girls! Come and see your new quarters, and this lovely kitchen."

"Isn't it beautiful? No wonder they call her The Mermaid, the name suits it, doesn't it?" Everyone had to agree.

"Who's the first one to make a cuppa?" Long silence fell in the room, all you could hear was the sea clashing against the boat, making the boat rock side side!

"I'll make tea," said Jane. "I'll be in charge of the kitchen."

"We'll take it in turns then" said Jean. Up till now she hadn't said much, she was overwhelmed by it all, still wasn't quite sure she wanted to do this, but it was too late to back out now, she said to herself. She went down below to help Jane with

the tea, the things hadn't been put away yet, but that would wait till later; they went up top just in time to hear the radio that the boys had got working.
"That sounds clear enough, at least we can make contact if we need to" Jane said.
"Well, that's what it's there for, dear" laughed Ben.
"Is everything away downstairs?" said Bill. "In another hour we ought to be on our way."
"No, there's still the food to be put in the cupboards; we didn't think we would be moving quite so soon, did we, Jean?"
"No, would have loved to stay a bit longer."
"Well, the sooner we move on the better," said Bill.
"Aye, aye, captain! We take it you are the captain now?"
"Well, yes, someone's got to be in charge and Ben and I discussed it last night, didn't we, Ben?"
"Yes, we did" said Ben.
"Right then, Jane, in that case we had better obey the captain, otherwise he will get us scrubbing the floors next." That made them smile, little did they know what was in store for them. It wasn't going to be all plain sailing, anyway time will tell. Ben went back to his duties and Bill went back to the radio to get the shipping forecast. The radio was telling them the weather and time of sail, the girls were busy putting away the food and cases; soon it was all ship shape as they say.
"Right, everyone, we're on our way at last! You can come on top if you want to, girls, I'll not bite!"
"There are a lot of boats; will we be able to pass them all?"
"Of course we will, that's what the shipping channels are for, to give us clearance."
"Oh, I see," said Jane. "How far do you think we will get this afternoon?"
"Well, if the weather holds with a bit of luck, should be somewhere near Santa. If the weather holds we can down anchor and do some exploring. What do you say about that?"
"Well, if you're sure, it would be quite exciting, don't you think, Jane?"
"Oh, yes, let's do that."
However it was late in the afternoon when they arrived at the island, when you got nearer to it you could here the animals: the birds were the noisiest. It was quite breezy and it had a kind of eerie feel about the place, it all looked as though people had not been there for some years. They put the boat along the edge and after collecting some of the things they thought they would need and also some emergency supplies set off to explore. Overhead you could hear the habitat, but other than that all was quite; no one was on the island, that was for sure. As they went further in, it came apparent it was empty, there was no one in sight, so they were alone on the island, which was a bit scary but as they had each other they weren't entirely alone, but little did they know what was in store for them. As they got further in, they found a cave, it was large enough for all of them so they decided to make this their home, as who knows how long they would be there? The weather was gaining on them by the hour, it looked as though they might have to stay on the island all night. Once they got their act together it didn't seem too bad. Inside

the cave it was quite dark but it actually felt quite cool, the walls were built of slate. There was water coming from the ceiling but it didn't feel damp as you would have thought.
Ben, being a scout master in his day, said they could build a fire. They had brought with them plenty of supplies, at least for a few days, and when the weather improved they would be on their way, or so they thought, they hadn't realized that some one else was on the island but alone, and had lived on there for a few years.
Ben and Bill lit the fire, which was soon burning. The girls went to fetch water, and soon they were all eating a hearty meal.
"That was good," said Ben. "It shows we hadn't forgotten what the boys scout taught us, what do you say Bill?!"
"You're right," said Bill. "That was a good meal, now the next thing is to do make up a bed for the night. We had better keep the fire going in case of unwanted animals. You never know what's on this island, we can't be too careful: we have to take care of the girls, that's our first priority."
"Yes, I think you're right for once; with Jane being the most adventurous one they can get up to all sorts of things. Well, anyway, let's sort the bedroom.
"I for one don't intend to stay here more than it's necessary" said Bill.
"Neither do I," replied Ben. "But we might as well make our stay comfortable."
"We're just going to go further into the cave, Ben, we shan't be long."
"OK, but be careful; you don't know who you might meet."
So off the girls went; all you could hear was the trickling of water coming down from the cave walls, every so often bats were flying around which made the girls jump. However they soon got used to them. What seem like an age, they suddenly realized they had gone too far. They couldn't help noticing that the walls were made of black slate and that the water had made icicles in all different shapes, on one side there were carvings of animals of every type.
"Someone must have been on this island to make these, they don't make them themselves" said Jean.
"No, I agree, they don't. Come on, let's get back to the boy's, it's beginning to feel a bit eerie.
Wait," said Jane. "We're not far from the end, there's light there and I can hear the waves from the sea bed, can you hear them?"
"I can now, the sea sounds quite rough, let's take a look."
"This island stretches for miles and look! There are coconuts and fir trees, some lizards..."
"Oh, look, there's one right near your feet!"
"Oh, where?" said Jane jumping up and down, making the leaves rattle. "Let's go round the corner and we might get to the boys that way, instead of going all the way back."
"Good idea! Come on, let's go."
"It will soon be getting dark, I wonder if the boys have sorted our beds out?
"I wonder what we will be sleeping on," laughed Jane.
"I don't really care, I am dead on my feet" remarked Jean. "I can't wait to see the boys."

Just as they turned the corner, Jane spotted something, she was not sure what it was.
"Let's hide behind this tree," said Jane. "I think we have company."
"Oh my goodness!" exclaimed Jean. "Who or what on earth is that?"
"It looks like one of those cave men you see on films, I wonder if he speaks English. Wait a minute, he's coming over to us, don't let him see were afraid."
"So you thought you were on your own on my island, didn't you? I've been here for 6 years and you're the first people I've had apart from some fishermen that have gone, of course, is that what you have done?"
"Em, well," muttered Jane. "Sort of, I am not sure! There are two more of us at the far end of the cave. I'm afraid we got carried away with ourselves. I don't suppose you know where we can find them? We are rather tired and thirsty."
"Actually you are not very far from them, you don't have to go all the way back."
"Thank goodness for that," they said together. "How far are we?"
"I'll take you" he said; he had a funny look on his face.
Jane and Jean looked at each other, wondering whether to trust him or not. Still, they had nothing to lose, did they? All too soon they could see the boys with a sigh of relief! And rushed over to them. When the boys looked up they saw their faces and immediately knew something was wrong.
"Goodness you two! Where have you been? We were just coming to look for you both, you look as though you have seen a ghost!"
It was quite a while before the girls could speak.
"We have company," murmured Jane. "Look!"
"Goodness, I was only joking when I said you might find a caveman; I didn't expect you to find one literary."
"We didn't, he actually found us. We went further in the caves than we thought and found him at the end of the caves, and he brought us back to you. He has been on this island a very long time, so he tells us."
"Oh, he does speak our language then," said Bill. "Has he lost his tongue? He looks a funny sort of fellow."
It was Bill who spoke first: "We are sorry to have invaded your island, we have a boat tied up near the shore, we will only be here a few nights and then we will be off. Is that OK with you, old chap?"
It was quite a while before he spoke and again with a funny accent: "You people are welcome to stay, we are in for some bad weather and I don't think your boat will stand it. My hut is way over the other side, you are most welcome to eat with me tomorrow night if you want to. I am afraid my hut is too small for all of you to sleep in, but eating is no problem.
"Have a good night, see you tomorrow. I am pleased to see you have kept the fires going."
"Bye for now," with that he picked up his spear and walked away.
"Let's go and see what the boys have done in the cave. Well, I never look here, Jane."
"Hammocks look very comfortable too," said Jane sounding quite surprised. "Who thought of that then? It's a very good idea. Who is going to be the one to try it?"
"You can" laughed Bill.

"OK," said Jane. "I will."
With no more ado she scrabbled in, but straight away fell out the other side.
"Ah! You can laugh, it's not as easy as it looks," cried Jane. "Let Jean try now. Well, well, who would have thought it? You have done this before, haven't you?"
"Well, yes actually I have."
"Oh, do tell" said Jane.
"Well, I used to go to brownies and I became a leader; we had to go on a survival course, we never had tents in those days as the war was on, you know! There were 6 in our group and each one had to show what skills they were good at, as it happen I was good at make shift sleeping arrangements and we made hammocks just like these. But I think these are stronger than mine, so of course this comes easy to me, once you get the hang of it, believe me, you will sleep well tonight. Also, we will keep the fire burning, that will keep us warm. Good idea of Ben to use barks from the trees, the boys have done well, don't you think Jane?"
"Yes, they have, I take my hats off to them if I had one." "
Is there any more coffee going? I am thirsty" said Jean.
"I think so, here you are. What about you, Jane?"
"No, it will keep me awake, if I have to sleep in these things I shall need something stronger. It's getting quite late, so I think we had better turn in, it's going to be a long night."
"I don't know about you, but it's strange, somehow I feel safer now we know someone else is on the island. Don't the rest of you feel the same?"
"Funny thing, we do," they all said. "At least we know someone is watching over us, now can we all get to sleep."
Before Bill went to bed he had one last look around and put some more bark on the fire; it wasn't long before he was asleep. The wind was getting up and the trees were waving their branches about, which had a soothing effect to the brain, soon Ben too went into a deep sleep. It was soon morning they all woke up the same time as each other. Ben and Bill were preparing breakfast, which they bought back from the boat.
"I'm afraid there is no more bread or bacon left, or milk."
"Oh, dear," said Jane. What are we going to do then?"
"Well, it looks like we shall have to live of the land, and make the most of it."
"Yes, that's all very well saying that, but we have no experience doing that, have we?"
"I have some which I learnt when I was a boy scout" said Ben feeling proud of himself.
"Well, you had better start eating your words if we are going to survive on this island" said Jane.
"What's on the menu tonight? Fish and chips?"
"I don't know about chips, but I think I could rustle up some fish."
"This I've got to see" said Bill.
"Let's see if we can find a thin long piece of bark, or wood would be better, and what can we use for net?"
They found odds and ends on the beach, and all of a sudden Jane screamed: "Look what I've found, will this do?"

"Jane, you're a marvel! It's just the very thing. Let's go down now and have a go at catching our dinner. I hope the fish are biting today; keep your fingers crossed, everybody, here we go."
"Pull up, pull up!" they all shouted at once. "Gosh this one's a big one! Take the hook out of its mouth and let's have a look at it."
"I think there's enough here for two people; can you catch about two more? And that should be enough for tonight, Ben. I'll take my hat off to you if I had one." They all started to laugh, life wasn't that bad on the island after all, at least they saw the funny side of things. Fortunately the weather had lessened and the wind had dropped, that's why they had caught the fish so quickly, it was going to be a good day after all. When they got back to the cave, they had a visitor waiting for them; in their excitement they had forgotten all about him.
"Hello," they said together. "We have been doing a bit of fishing, hope you don't mind. It's your island after all, but we had to do something so we can have dinner tonight."
They all held their breath waiting for him to speak, what seemed a long time, finally he spoke: "Very good you, catch fish" he said. "You have very good one too, who made that?" he said to Jane.
"My husband made it, he was in the scouts when he was younger."
"Ben smiled at him and started to say something, when the man came up to him and said: "Yes, very good, my man, but later I'll show you how to hunt wild boar, we have a few on here but they go in hiding, so we have to watch out for them."
Bill spoke up then and told him they won't be on the island much longer: "As soon as this wind dies down, then we shall be off, thanks all the same."
"That's as maybe, but in the meantime you have to eat, too much fish is not good for you, you know, the girls can collect coconuts and you can crack those and get the milk from them, they are full of protein."
So that's what they were doing late in the afternoon, it had been a glorious day, at last the sun was coming out. They all went back to the caves, when the old man said to them: "Tonight you have supper with me? I cook fish."
"Thank you, you're most kind, we will be there. Bye for now then" said Jane and Jean together.
The afternoon went by quickly, Jane and Jane collected coconuts for the milk, it did not taste too bad in the coffee and tea. With the coconuts they made a soft mixture and added some milk to make a pudding, which to their amazement was very tasty to the palate, and quite refreshing. The girls also found some berries which they did exactly the same as the coconut. To their amazement they were getting the hang of this survival thing quite well. That evening they found themselves sitting around the old mans fire, the smell of the fish was quite something, they had rice too, all washed down with berry fruit. He was telling them how he came to be on the island, all those years ago. He had a small boat just like them and one day the weather had turned on him. He hadn't intended to stay this long but as time went by he got kind of got used to being on his own, so he decided to stay; and all the animals became his friends, the ones he liked best were the monkeys, he knew most of them. Some times they helped him to find food, so he never really felt alone. In the early years

on the island there had been some fishermen with their trawlers; they would land near the shore and they never used to stay long, and they never really bothered him.
"Do you ever want to go back to the real world, Joshua?" As by now they were on first name terms.
"No, not really, although I might one day, who knows?"
"Would you like to come back with us?" said Jane suddenly. Ben and Bill looked at her thinking she had gone quite mad, what was she thinking of asking him that sought of question? She knew Ben didn't like him. There was a long silence, then he spoke: "That's very kind of you, my dear, but no, thanks, I shall properly spend the rest of my life on this island. You see, I have no one else in my life so I might as well stay here. There is one thing I want you all to promise me, that you will not let anyone know I am here. Please, I beg you all."
"Of course we won't, will we guys?"
"No," they all said at once. "Not if you don't want us to, but what if you become ill? Then what will happen to you?"
Joshua thought for a moment: "Well, I have been lucky, so far I have just had a few colds, but nothing to worry about, so here hoping my luck will hold for a few years to come yet. Now let's all cheer up and have our last drink of the day! Now we are friends, at last things should be more fun even if it is for a short while."
"Thank you for tonight and all the stories you have told us, you are a very brave man indeed" said Jane, and Jean had to agree with her. The men said nothing, they were going to talk to Jane when they got back to their cave.
Joshua gave them some food to help them over for a few days, said good night and walked in silence to the cave, which wasn't far away. When they arrived the fire was still burning. Bill went to get some more wood as the nights were getting quite chilly now, all was quite apart from the birds and the monkeys jumping high in the trees, also the squirrels. Bill and Ben didn't get chance to talk to Jane as the girls went straight to bed, only Bill and Ben stayed up, they were going to discuss about leaving the island as soon as the weather changed, hoping it wouldn't be too long, as sleeping in the beds didn't do much for their bodies, and they really wanted to get home: it had been a longer adventure than they anticipated.
"We will give it one more week, Bill, shall we? Then we will be on our way."
"Yes, I think that would be a good idea. I think Jane is getting too attached to our cave friend, don't you think so, Ben?"
"Yes, I do, fancy her asking him to come back with us, as it is he hasn't really got any thing to go back to, I feel sorry for him. But one thing that's bothering me is why doesn't he want us tell anyone he his on the island?"
"I was thinking the same, it makes you wonder if he does have anything to hide. No doubt the mystery will resolve itself sooner or later."
"Anyway we can not do much about it so I am going to turn. Have a good night, Bill, see you in the morning."
Despite a very restless night Ben woke up in a good mood, he felt that today would get them on their way, he couldn't wait to get home to Bouncer, whom he missed terribly. Nevertheless he was getting fed up with this island and he wanted to be on

his way as soon as possible, just see if he doesn't. After breakfast he went in search of his friend Joshua to see if he thought they could be on the move; he was hoping the news would be good. When he found him by the edge of the sea, catching fish again, he thought if he had any more fish he would go mad; it was supposed to be good for you, he knew that, but you can have too much of a good thing.
"Well, hello there, young man." He always called him that, he hated it. "What can I do for you? And where are the others?"
"They are having breakfast. I just wanted to know if we can make plans for leaving this island. Have you got any more weather forecast information?"
"Getting tired of the open air or you're not the adventurous type, are you?"
"Never mind what I am. Can you get us off here soon, say in a few days?"
"Well, now, let's see; yes, the weather has changed quite a bit, I must say, but there is still quite a bit of wind about and I don't think your boat would stand it. I suggest you wait a few more days. Life's not to bad on here surely?"
"Well, that's your opinion, I for one like my home comforts," and with that he walked back to his party, to tell them the news. *I don't know how they will react to it.*
When he arrived near the cave, they were all busy collecting fire wood; it was late October and the nights were drawing in. It was really time they set for home, he was in a thoughtful mood when Jane approached him, she was worried: never before had she seen him look like this, very downcast and with a worried look on his face.
"Goodness me, Ben, what ever the matter, what has Joshua been saying to you?"
"Not what he has been saying to me that's bothering me, Jane, love. I was asking him when does he think we can get off this unforeseen island, and do you know what he said?"
"No, do tell me, I am all ears" said Jane.
"Well, he went on about how the boat wouldn't hold up against these winds, he felt it would be dangerous to go on, till they die down, which could been another week on here, which I couldn't really bear, as I just want to get home to Bouncer."
"Yes, dear, we all do, but don't you think it would be wise to go by what Joshua says? After all he knows about these shores better than we do. I would be far happier to go along with what he says, Ben, dear. Oh, do not look so sad! Don't worry, we will be off here as soon as the weather permits."
"Well, as long as I keep you safe, darling, that's all that matters. Shall we see if there is any more tea on the bone fire stove?"
Arm in arm they walked back to the others, they had gathered enough wood for the day so they were able to relax for the rests of the afternoon. It was a quite day, hardly any wind that Joshua was talking about."
"You know, dear," said Ben. "He might be wrong after all."
"Don't count your chickens too soon," said Bill. "He's always been right so far and I for one would prefer to wait to see what the weather will be doing. We don't want the boat to upturn in the wind, I think it can get quite strong in these parts."
"Oh, now who's the expert all of a sudden! You have never been in these parts before."

"No, I haven't, but I looked it up on the Internet before we came out. It mention the winds can get quite strong especially this time of year."
"Well, never mind that, now we have more important things to worry about too."
"Like what for?" said Ben still in a mood.
"Oh, Ben, snap out of this moody mood, please, we can't help the weather, but as Jane was saying, there are other things on our minds. What are we doing for dinner later? That's what we want to know."
"If I have any more fish I shall start to smell all fishy, and then Jane won't have anything more to do with me."
"If you don't stop being so moody I won't anyway. Why don't you go for a nice long walk? It will do you good."
"Yes, maybe, I will see you all later, bye for now."
"Goodness me! I've never seen him so down as this," said Bill. "The sooner we get home the better."
In the end they all had to make with fish as that's what they had left. There was still some tea left, which was most welcoming . Hours later Ben arrived back, he had cheered up no end, much to the relieve of the others.
"What you got there?" said Jane. "You have been to the boat, haven't you?"
"Yes, I've been searching the cupboards and found some more coffee and some tins of stuff that we like."
"The boat's still intact, I take it" said Bill.
"Oh, yes, it's fine; I think it's a bit lonely without us though."
"Now, now, don't get all sad again, Ben, at least we have some provisions for the moment."
As they were talking they didn't notice the weather changing: it was getting quite windy, and the trees were swaying about, the dark clouds were forming and down came the rain; lucky for them they were in the cave and had the fire going which kept them warm and the fish smelt quite good too. Jane wondered what all the fuss was about fish was a lovely dish to set up. They were having their dinner when all of a sudden there was a loud bang!! It made them all jump.
"Goodness, that hit something."
"I know," said Bill. Alarmed, Ben looked at Bill; each knew what the other one was thinking. Without alarming the girls they knew what they had to do once the rain had stopped. It grew dark quite quickly so they decided to wait till the morning. They made the light by using a burning stick made from the wood from the trees, and put them on the wall; it also helped to keep them warm. When they had all had their dinner they went further into the caves to shield themselves from the rain and wind.
Ben was sorry he was rude to Joshua but somehow he just didn't like him, nor trust him, although he couldn't really say why. *Some people are like that*, he thought. Neither of them had a good night, and were very quiet in the morning. Bill and Ben were nowhere to be found when the girls got up, so they put some more wood on the fire, mostly to keep the animals at bay and keep them warm. The men arrived at the boat, who should be there? It was Joshua, he had the same idea as them.

"You heard the big bang then, Joshua, and you had the same idea as us? What do you reckon has it been hit?"
"We shall not know till we get inside to start her up."
So that's what they did; much to everyone's relieve it started first time. They checked it over and it was all in tacked. The storm went as quickly as it came and it turned out to be a calm day, not warm but at least it was quiet.
"How you coping for food? Have you plenty of firewood?" said Jose.
Ben said they were OK, thanks, then he said it they would like to join him for supper later.
"Thanks," they said. "We would well bring some coffee with us too."
"Thank you, that would be most kind. I have not had coffee in a long time."
"No, I bet you have not, mate" said Bill, and they walked back to their makeshift hotel; they were beginning to feel like cavemen themselves.
As the days went by Ben was getting more and more restless and moody, snapping at every one in his path. Jane was getting quite worried about him. *If we don't get him home soon he will make himself ill.*
Jean noticed how quiet Jane was and asked her what was wrong, was she ill?, she wondered. Jane went to find Joshua to see what he could do and get the weather report, which was good news anyway; that should cheer him up at least, he said in a few days it would be OK to set sail but first they had to go and check out the boat.
"Tell Ben and Bill to meet me there later, Jane."
So with that, feeling excited again, she went back to find the boys, who were in deep discussion on when they were going to leave. The weather was a lot calmer of late, not knowing when it will change they thought it's now or never. When Jane came back she told them what Joshua said.
"OK, we'll go later.
"He said can you meet him at the boat?"
"Yes, no problem."
Late in the afternoon they went to meet Joshua, who was there waiting for them.
"Right," he said. "Let's check out the boat. I've made a list of all the important things to do, it will be easier that way. Who's the captain?"
"I am" said Bill.
"Go up deck and check oil and diesel and radio. Ben here can check food supplies, etc."
"I thought I was in charge of this boat" said Bill.
"Never mind," said Ben. "Go with him for a moment, otherwise he might keep us on this island a bit longer."
"OK, I guess you're right, Ben, a few more hours won't hurt."
"I can't wait to get underway, can you?"
"No," said Bill. "Neither can I."
"Who knows? By tomorrow we should be on our way, weather permitting."
"You're right, it all depends on that really."
Everything what Joshua told them to do was done, they went back to report all was well with The Mermaid.

"Well done," he said. "Soon you will be on your way, as this might be your last night with me. Why don't you have supper with me?"
"Thank you, that's most kind of you. Then we can thank you properly for helping us to survive in this God's forsaken place."
"Oh, come on, it hasn't been that bad surely; I've taught you a few tricks, don't you think?"
"Yes, I grant you that, but it's miles and miles from nowhere, surely you can't survive on here for years."
"Well, I've been on here for what? It must be about 6 years that I can remember."
"Are you planning to stay on this island indefinitely?"
"I'm not sure," he said. "But it will be some time yet before I leave."
With that he walked back to his hut, looking like a very lost soul indeed. Ben almost felt sorry for him, but he couldn't really take to the man at all, he couldn't quite put a finger on it, he just felt very uneasy around him. The boys went back to the girls, they were busy preparing to nights dinner.
"Put those away," said Ben. "We have all been invited over to Joshua's tonight, as this might be our last supper with him. We have checked the boat and it's ready for the sea, with Joshua telling us what to do."
"Yes, you should have seen Ben's face, he wasn't a very happy bunny, were you Ben?"
"No, I wasn't. We're in charge of our Mermaid, anyone would think it was his boat, not ours."
"Never mind, love," said Jane. "We'll soon be away from here and soon we will all see Bouncer. I wonder how he's got on with John."
"Knowing him he will be spoiling him, he was telling me that he might be getting one himself."
"Oh, wouldn't that be nice for Bouncer? He loves being around other dogs, doesn't he?"
"Yes, he does," said Jean, who at this point hadn't said a word. "Bouncer's a lovely dog, I shouldn't mind one like him either."
"That might not be a bad idea," said Bill. "I like dogs and if we can get one like Bouncer that would be great. It will also give you exercise, which I think we both need." Bill winked at Ben. "What do you think, Ben?"
"Em, keep me out of this," said Ben laughing. "You make your own minds up what you do."
"Yes, Ben's right, but I do think it would be good for you both" said Jane.
"Well, we'll see when we get home, if we get home in one peace, we've a long way to go yet."
They heard the signal that Joshua was ready for them, so they put some more wood on the fire and kept the torches alight for later.
"That was a good thing we set up, you know, having a signal to call us for supper, Josh?"
"Yes, clever, wasn't it? When you've gone I shall keep it for further use. Who knows when I might need it? If I see a boat or ship near these shores they would hear it, and come in to investigate."

"I was fishing this morning, and I caught some crab and lobster, some other types of fish, so you have a good choice."
"You've done well," said Jane. "Was it easy to cock them on your make shift fire?"
"Yes, quite easy, didn't take long at all."
"It certainly smells good," said Ben. "Can't wait to try that crab, anyway here's the coffee."
"Oh, good," said Josh. "Haven't had coffee in years, thank you everyone. I'm going to miss you all, you've been very kind to me."
"Well, you can still come back with us, you know, it's not too late, is it Bill?"
Bill didn't quite know what to say, he was looking at Ben's face, he almost knew the answer without even thinking about it.
It was Joshua who answered first: "I think I will stay here a bit longer, thanks all the same. I'll be OK, don't you worry about me! Just you make sure you get home safely, that's all."
"OK, if you're sure; now let's make a toast to a safe passage home."
"Hear, hear!!" they all shouted, making the animals in the trees move.
Then they left it, tomorrow, they will be on their way. With joy in their hearts they went back to the cave, that night there was no wind, in fact it felt rather eerie odd somehow, but they didn't know why; anyway it didn't matter. Nothing was going to stop them now, a few hours from then they would be at sea. Hurray! Before they went to bed they made sure everything was ship shape ready for going, they were all pretty exhausted but it was a job that had to be done; the last thing they did was to sort out the fires and the torches. That night they dreamt of Bouncer and the home ward journey, they hoped they didn't have too much trouble awaiting them, it had been an unforgettable experience to say the least. Ben for one would like to forget.

The long journey home

At last the day arrived. They had their last breakfast, made sure all the fires were out and went down to the boat. It was sitting so proud near the edge of the sea, it was as if it knew it was going home! Jane and Jean went down below, everything looked the same, it looked as though it had survived the winds after all.
"Gosh, isn't it nice to be on board?" said Jane.
"Yes, it is" replied Jean.
"Is everyone ready? Then were on our way at last."
It was late afternoon when they set sail, on there way home at last. Bill was sailing The Mermaid, which was behaving very well, it was doing about 20 knots and very smooth, the weather was behaving itself too, so by very late evening they made good progress. Bill said he estimated they should be in their waters and heading for home.

Jane said that the boat was very good, you could hardly feel it at all, not like the first time, she was everywhere. It was going to be a long night, the girls tried to relax but were still feeling on edge.
"He was a funny sort of chap, wasn't he?" Bill said.
"Yes, but he was a dap hand in the kitchen" Ben said.
In no time at all the island soon disappeared and the girls went down below with a sad heart; it was lunch time when Ben came down to them. He was quite tired.
"I am off to bed now, Jane, if I am going to do the night watch. The weather is quite good at the moment so Bill should be alright, but can you keep an eye on him, please, Jean? Good night girls."
Jean went up to see Bill: "What knots are we doing?"
"About 12, I think," Bill said. "I could murder for a coffee if we have any."
"OK, captain coffee coming up" said Jane laughing.
"That's better, Jean, I don't like you looking so sad. This will be a good trip home, I think I can feel it in my bones."
"Let's hope so we have had enough disasters on this trip."
Jean went down below, make Bill's coffee and sandwiches. Jane was busy putting things away.
"Do you want a drink, Jane?"
"Oh, yes, please. Isn't it nice and quiet, Jean? No more animal noises and creepy crawlies and snakes. I can't wait to get home."
Jean went up top to get Bill his dinner. Ben was still fast asleep soon it will be his turn. They had been at sea about 6 hours and the sun was going down. They had dinner and had coffee while Jane washed up.
"Well, everyone, I am off to bed see, you in the morning."
Ben wondered if they could get on the radio to contact their families.
"I don't know," said Jane. "I will go and ask Bill to give it a try." Off she went humming to herself. "Bill, can you make contact on the radio? Ben wants to know."
"I can but try," Bill said, "here let's give it a go."
The radio gave out some weird sounds but nothing came through, they tried for about an hour to no avail.
"Dead as a doe so that means we can not get the shipping forecast either. Afraid it's bad news, tell Ben we are not out of the woods yet. We'll try when we get further along the coast, we have not far to go. Can you tell Ben to take over? I am in need of refreshments."
"OK, will do," said Jane.
"Oh, by the way, it's nice to see you have cheered up a bit," said Bill. "It won't be long before were home and dry.
When Ben saw Bill he mentioned about the radio.
"We shall just have to pray the weather holds, that's all."
Jane went into see Ben who by now had fallen fast asleep.
"He is sound on," she told Jean. "We're going to have a job to wake him, he looks so peaceful."
"Oh, dear," said Jean. "He has had a rough time of it lately."

"I know," said Jane. "So have we all."
"He didn't like Josh very much, did he?"
"No, poor old Josh. I wonder what he is doing now, I miss him, you know."
"Yes, I know you do but I have a feeling we shall be seeing him again once we get home."
"Oh, do you really think so?"
"I think so" said Jean.
The girls went to the kitchen to see what they had got for dinner.
"Not bad," said Jane. "How does stewed steak sound?"
"And mixed tin potatoes and vegetables, that will please the boys," said Jean. "Let's start cooking."
It wasn't long before Bill shouted down to Jane: "That dinner smells good! Save some for me please!"
Jane and Jean laughed: "I knew it would get their taste buds going!"
Then they heard Ben's voice: "Goodness now we have to of them wanting dinner!"
"It will be ready in 10 minutes" the girls said.
"Good," said Ben. "I am starving."
"So am I," said the other.
"Men and their stomach; what do you say, Jean?"
"Yes, I will agree with you there. Now let's get this on the table whilst it hot. Bill had better have his up top, otherwise the boat might go astray, it's behaving itself so far."
So Ben took it up to him.
"It's not a bad night," said Bill. "Clear as day, not much wind though, still we should be OK. I will try to contact the shipping channel in the morning."
"OK," said Ben. "Good idea, you're good at this, Bill."
"This dinner is good, Ben," said Bill. "The girls have done well in the circumstances."
"I think Jane is missing Josh. I overheard them talking in the kitchen when I woke up."
"Eavesdropping were you? Naughty, naughty boy" said Bill teasing.
"Well, at least were got our sense of humour back."
"Why, yes we have. Well, I'll be a monkey's uncle." And they were still laughing when Jane came up.
"It's good to hear you boys in good sprites again, especially you, Ben, you've been like a bear with a sore head."
"I have not, have I, Bill?"
"Well, maybe a bit, my friend."
"Anyone for tea?" said Ben.
"Yes, please," they all said. "That would be nice."
"OK, back in a moment."
After they had their tea, Ben went to take over from Bill, who was still on about the dinner.
"Everything's OK up here, Ben kept it steady at about 20 k. We should be OK at that, any problems give me a shout."
"Aye, aye!"

"Now then that's enough of that" said Bill.
Ben looked ahead of him, it certainly was a beautiful night; he felt quite relax but wished the thing would go faster, he wanted to get home as soon as he can. All was quiet down below, everyone must be asleep; at least they will get a good night's sleep from now on. The boat was swaying a bit the wind was getting up, he pulled up his heavy coat and lit his pipe. He hadn't had it for a while, he didn't take it with him on the island.
It was certainly a long night, suddenly he heard a crackling noise: "Goodness, I had forgotten all about the radio! Right, let me see." He picked up the mike and spoke very clearly. "Hello, hello! Mermaid Enterprise here, what is the problem?"
"Hello, this is the shipping channel. What speed are you doing at the moment?"
"About 20 k., why?"
"Well, there is a big storm brewing and it's coming your way, just slow down a bit and you should be alright."
"Thanks for the warning, over and out."
With that the radio went silence again. Ben didn't like the sound of it, and he looked at his watch. *Oh, dear*, he said to himself, *a few more hours yet to go if we can just make it round this bay we might be OK*. A few more hours passed; suddenly a big crack of thunder and a flash of lighting. *Goodness, that one was close, louder than the one on the island. I bet it's waken them up down below*, but no there wasn't a sound from them. Ben felt really alone. It didn't bother him too much about the storm; he had been in worse ones when he was in the army, that was a long time ago. A few more hours went bye, the sun was coming out over the horizon, the sky was of a red colour and the wind was fair to middling. It looked a very pretty sight.
He could hear movement down below, and he heard Bill's voice: "Morning, Ben, had a good night?"
"It's been good," said Ben. "I had a message on the radio earlier about a bad storm brewing up, but I think it must have gone round us."
"Thank goodness for that," said Bill. "I did hear the thunder though, but I was so tired I went back to sleep."
"Never mind, it's done you good, we shouldn't be long before we turn round the next corner; then it's straight up towards home."
"That sounds like music to my ears" said Bill.
"And mine" said Ben.
Jean brought up some tea and a few sandwiches.
"They look good," said Ben. "I was getting hungry."
"About another 2 days and we should be home and dry. Let's hope the weather holds" said Jean. She went down below to see Jane, who was deep in her book, she had been reading it for days.
"My, that looks like a good book," said Jean. "What's it all about then?"
"I will tell you when I've finished" she said; she looked up at Jean and sighed, then went back to reading. So Jean went to the kitchen to see what supplies they had left, when all of a sudden a very loud bang was heard.
"Goodness me!" she cried. What was that?"

Jane came to her.
"Are you alright?" said Jean.
"I am, but what about the boys? Can you go up and see what's wrong?"
"Of course, I'll give you a shout if I need you!"
"OK," said Jane. "I shall not be long."
Jane went up, and by the look on the boys' faces she could tell it didn't look good.
"Well, whatever happened, is it bad news Ben? Well, will some one tell me what's up?"
"We think we have hit a rock or something, whatever it was it sounded jolly hard. I think it's what they call in sailing run a ground."
"Goodness, that does sound serious."
"Yes, I'm afraid it is; in other words were stranded."
"Oh, dear, I'll better go and tell Jean." So she went down and gave her the bad news.
"Oh, dear," she said. "Now what are we going to do? We're right in the middle of nowhere, and it's getting cold too. Well, let's see what the boys are doing about it, shall we?"
"Yes, let's" said Jane.
They went up to Ben and Bill: "Well, how are we going to fix this then, Ben?"
"Well, Bill here suggests we put some sort of signal out. Who knows? There might be a ship passing our way."
"Pigs might fly," said Jane.
"Well, there could be," said Bill. "We can all but try; let's get some torches going and keep all the lights on the boat as long as we have still got power, but I don't know for how long. We'll keep one torch handy, the rest we can use. Pity this has happened, we're safe as long as the weather holds."
It was almost dark and the boat looked really good with all its lights on it.
"Feels like Christmas has come early" said Jane.
"It looks alive" laughed Jane.
"Yes, I suppose you could say," that chimed in Bill. "Anyway we're safe for the moment; the sea is quite calm."
"Let's hope it stays that way" said Ben, sounding very worried indeed.
"Now don't start getting moody again, you're happier when things go well aren't you, Ben?" said Jane.
"Yes, dash it all so does every one here."
"That's right, we all do, now I think it's time we all turn in and try and get a good night's sleep."
"It won't be easy" said Ben.
"Oh, you kill joy," laughed Jane. "Come on, let's get to bed."
Soon they were all sounding asleep. They woke up rather late. Jane went into the kitchen first to see if she had enough power to make some breakfast; surprisingly she had and when the others joined, her breakfast was well under way.
"Goodness," said Bill. "You don't mess about, do you?"
"No," said Jane. "I was getting hungry."
"So was I" said Jean. "I did not mean to sleep in so long, but after those beds on the island I was too comfortable to move."

"You can say that again but once you got used to them they were OK."
"I wonder how Josh is getting on without us; I felt sorry we had to leave him behind."
"Yes, but we tried our best to get him to come, didn't we?" said Jean. "Who knows? We might see him again one day." Little did she know how true her words were.
It was going to be a long day. Bill and Ben prepared things for a long wait, they organized lights to go on top of the boat so any ship would be able to see them, they also tried to keep cheerful for the sake of the girls. At least they had enough food to last them a few days thanks to Josh. Ben thought to himself that maybe he wasn't such a bad chap after all, but even with those thoughts he still didn't like him, he just hoped he wouldn't be seeing him again, but neither Ben knew what laid ahead. Ben went down to the kitchen and told the girls to get some rest, at the moment the sea was being kind to them but as Ben knew on these shores the weather could change. All they could do was waiting and praying that their signal was heard before it shut down on them. *What did Jane say? This was going to be a trouble free trip. If only...* said Ben to himself.
"I'll take first watch if you like," said Bill. "You girls get a good night's sleep while the sea is behaving itself."
"OK," the girls said together. "Thanks very much, but we will do our share of ship watching."
"That's alright," said Bill. "No need to worry about that, just keep yourselves as calm as you can."
"Well, we will say goodnight then, make sure you get some rest too."
At about 3 in the morning the weather started to turn: it was raining hard and the wind got up again, lucky they bought some heavy bags so they were able to keep dry. The hot tea and the soup which Jane had made them earlier helped. She was such a thoughtful girl, thought Ben, he wouldn't know what he would do without her. At the moment they were quite safe. Bill and Ben had taken it in turns during the night and in the morning the weather had change again; it was a glorious sunrise, the colours shown orange and red. Bill went down to see the girls were OK, he found them in the kitchen.
"Something smells good," said Ben. "I'm starving."
"So am I" said Bill.
"Oh, you men and your stomachs! It won't be long now. Did you have a good night, you two?"
"Apart from the weather it wasn't bad, that soup you made, Jane, was lovely, it kept the cold out. It was a good idea of yours, Jane."
"Oh I'm glad it helped, I don't suppose there was any sign of the ship?"
Ben laughed: "No, dear! Don't worry, if there was you would have heard the commotion and we would be on board and away by now."
"Well, let's hope we spot one today. I can't wait to get on dry land again" said Jane.
"Well, that goes for all of us, we shall just have to sit tight and wait. I am going to bed."
"I'll stay up for a few more hours," said Bill. "If there's anything happening I'll fetch you."

"OK," said Ben. "Thanks, see you later then, girls."
The girls went down to prepare dinner. The sun was just coming out; it looked like it was going to be a lovely day. They were in need of something to cheer them all up. Bill went up top and had another go with the radio; suddenly a crackling sound came from it which made him jump. At last he had radio contact: he quickly sent over a Mayday call; it was a very week signal, he could just make out the reply. Now all he had to do was waiting. He went down and told the girls at least there was some ray of hope: he didn't know how far the ship was from them as the signal was so week, but what it told him was that there was a ship somewhere near them. All they had to do was wait and keep a look out for it; at least it was a clear day, just hope it reaching them before nightfall. They need to be rescued soon before the food ran out, it would have to be fish again, and Ben had had enough of fish these past few weeks. The girls did a good job in the kitchen as to what little food they had, but they all wanted to get back on dry land. Late in the afternoon just after dinner Bill shouted down to them very excitedly.
"Did you hear that loud noise, everyone? There's a ship approaching us; they have sent us a message."
"Oh, what did they say?" they all said together.
"They are sending some dinghies out to us. We have to get things ready to take on board, we must make sure our boat is safe to leave."
"Oh, isn't this exciting" said Jane. She always loved an adventure and they were going to be saved after all. In the last few hours they were busy preparing to leave their boat, they made it as safe as they could. Outside they heard quite a commotion; there were shouts: "Ahoy there ship mates! How many are there of you?"
"Oh, there are only four of us but were very glad to see you."
"We're very pleased to help you," said one of the men. "We will help you get on board, hope you have got all your things."
"Yes, of course we have. We will have to get some one to rescue The Mermaid."
"Don't worry about it for the moment, let's get you lot sorted first, it later."
Once on board they were greeted by the ship's captain and all the other crew; they kept asking questions like: where have you come from and where was this island you keep talking about? It all sounded very exciting.
The captain took their names and checked their particulars. Everything was fine, captain Jim had a very strong voice; he sounded Irish but he was very friendly, he told them that they were not very far from one of the main shipping ports, they had about 10 days left before they reached it.
"That's good news," said Bill. "Is there anyway we can reach home?"
"And where's home?" said Jim.
"Oh, in Cartagena" said Ben.
"Lovely place," said Jim. "In fact some of my family live there too. In the morning we will try and reach them. The storm's just about blown itself out and we should have some good sailing weather from now on."
"The news just get better and better," said Bill. "We can't wait to get back on dry land again, it's been quite an adventure, I can tell you."

Jim went below and shown them to their cabins, at least they were dry and they could get a shower and shave, the boys by now had grown a beard and they were unrecognizable.
After a good supper they all turned in and slept well into the afternoon. Jim didn't mind as he said: "Coming on board you all looked pretty exhausted."
When they did eventually go up deck they looked a lot better.
"Ah, I see that sleep did you all good! Come and have something to eat, you must be starving."
"We are" they all said together, then they all had a hearty meal, the men had beer while the girls had wine, which went down a treat.
"Right," said Jim. "I have managed to get through to the port and they are trying to contact your family, later on I shall get a call back and then you can speak to them."
"Hurray!" they all shouted.
"Mind it will only be a quick call as we don't want to block the channel."
All to soon they were talking to their family, although being where they were the radio was cracker ling and the voices sounded so far away, which of course that's where they were so it wasn't surprising that they could not hear them, but at least they knew that they were safe and that what mattered. What seemed like ages, the conversation died away and then they were gone. On the way back to Jim they were very quiet, each with their own thoughts. Ben couldn't wait to get home to Bouncer.
"I wonder if he has forgotten us" said Ben to Jane.
"No, I don't think so; still it won't be long before we are in Cartagena. John might meet us there with him."
"I hope so" said Ben, and then he went in search of Jim.
"Hello," he said as Ben came up to him. Everything's alright in the home front then, old boy?!"
"Oh, don't you start calling me that, please, I had enough of it on the island."
"Sorry, didn't mean to offend, it just suits you, that's all."
"Well, no more, please."
"Now then," Jim said in a quiet voice, "what's all this about a man all alone on the island? Why has he been there all these years? That's what I would like to know, and why don't you like him? Because it's clear you don't.
"Well, Jim, it's like this, when we arrived on the island he kept saying that he didn't want anyone to know he was there and everything he did while we were there seemed very odd, always looking over his shoulder as they say. I just didn't trust him, that's all there is to it. Oh, also he had an eye on Jane, she was besotted by him, and that made it worse. Once we had a fishing competition to see who could catch the most fish, which I hate by the way, we had rather a lot of it, and Jane would show off in front of him and of course he liked that, so I am glad to see the back of him."
"Yes, you're right, he does sound like an odd chap; still you can relax now and enjoy the trip home. By the way, dinner will be about 8 tonight; is that OK for you?"
"Lovely," Ben said as long as it's not *fish*."
And that made Jim laugh. "That's a good one" and walked away to find his number one.

His number one was down below, on the radio. Jim could hear voices, they were telling them that there was some bad weather in their area and they should keep the radio on at all times in case of the weather gets worse. Jim told them that he was doing about 20 knots and asked them if that was OK.
"No problem there, captain but just be on your guard, over and out." Then it all went quiet. "Well, number one, what do you make of that? It looks like we are in for some rough weather."
"That's all we need as I know our new friends want to get home as fast as this ship will go. Never mind that now it's moving OK at the moment, so let's go into the kitchen to see how that's doing."
"Well, chef, how long will dinner be?"
"Oh, not long, captain, in about another 2 hours I would say."
"Good, I think our friends will be ready for it, hurry it up, there's a good chap."
"Aye, aye, captain, I'll see what I can do."
"Thanks, Bob, I'll see you later then." He went of to find Ben and his party to tell them about the dinner and the weather report.
Ben was in the quiet lounge while the rest of them were having a nap in their cabins. Ben took out his pipe and he had a beer at the side of him. *This is what holidays are all about*, he said to himself; just then Jim walked in.
"Now then, here you are, glad you are resting at last, it will do you good. Just come to tell you that dinner will be a bit later than as planned, also the weather report wasn't very good for this area, but saying that we are making good progress."
"Oh, that's all right, Jim, after all we are not going anywhere, not indirectly."
"Can I have a few words with you, Ben?"
"Of course, fire away. What's on your mind?"
"About this boat of yours I have contacted the arena where you got it from; they wanted to know exactly where it's moored so they can locate exactly where it is." Jim had bought his map with him and they spread it out on the lounge table.
"The area they were looking at was in San Nicolas and further up was the island; he did tell me the name of it. I shall have to ask Jane at dinner. Can we sort it out tomorrow, Jim, about the boat now when you make contact with them can I talk to them?"
"No problem, Ben, of course you can. I will see you at dinner then, bye for now; enjoy your rest, you look as though you need it."
It wasn't long before he was asleep, and he dreamt of Bouncer and the longing for home, never again would he go on an adventure with Jane, although it wasn't entirely her fault, bless her. All too soon the quietness was over the noise of the ship startled him. *Goodness me, what ever is going on I better go and see.*
When he came up deck the weather was going crazy: there was a gusty wind blowing and suddenly a loud crack of thunder, then lighting, the ship rolled from side to side. Ben saw Jim on the side board of the ship; he shouted to Ben to get down below, there wasn't any thing he could do and neither could he, they just had to wait till it blow itself out, for the moment the ship was OK and it could weather the storm as long as the waves were not to high.

When the storm ended, they went to have dinner together. At last the evening dragged on for a long time, one by one they dispersed. Bill stay behind to talk to Jim about The Mermaid, as he was in charge of the boat he had to notify the owners of her whereabouts. How he was going to tell he didn't quite know? The captain said he would help him, and so he did the next morning, so he thanked him for all his kindness and help he had given them.
"Don't mention it, Bill, it's been a pleasure meeting you all and I am only to glad they were safe."
They were to leave the ship at 13.00 hours the next day. There will be a transport waiting for them. They finished their coffee in the quiet lounge and they were discussing their next move. Ben could not understand why he wasn't invited to go with Bill to see the captain, after all he was part of the team, or so he thought. Perhaps Bill had other matters to speak to him about, he was soon to find out, Bill didn't think he was going to be pleased.
Jane told Bill that Ben wasn't happy about being left out of the meeting with Jim.
"I'll go and see him and put him in the picture now, and explain what happened; it will be alright, you'll see."
"I hope you're right."
"Hello there, Ben, how are you? I understand from Jane you are not very happy with me."
"You should have called me in when you went to see Jim."
"Sorry but there wasn't time; he was ranting on about the island and Joshua."
"Oh, not again, that man is becoming a pain. I shan't be sorry when this holiday's over!"
"Me neither, but listen, I have something important to tell you."
"OK, shoot, I'm all ears after all I've a lot to catch up on."
"Well, our friend Joshua is a wanted man."
"Oh, who wants him then?"
"No, straight up, he's wanted by the FBI!"
"What on earth for?!"
Bill took a sip of his coffee, cleared his throat, and told Ben that the captain had the FBI onto him about Joshua: "Apparently they caught some smuggles in one of the caves near Santa Pola about 4 months ago and they are looking for a fourth person involved; they believe he might be their man."
"Yes, but he has been on the island for years. I never saw any boat while we were there, did you?"
"No, I didn't, but he could have helped them to transport drugs some how, anyway the bottom line is they will want to speak to us later. I've got the address where we have to go properly in a few days time."
"Oh, my goodness! What are we going to tell the girls, Bill?"
"Well, there is nothing for it but tell them what we know."
"Jane will be devastated, you know how she feels about him."
"I know, but we can't let her think he is a Mr. Nice Guy, can we?"
"I don't think for one minute he's their man," said Ben.

"We will have to wait and see anyway. I am sorry for not taking you with me to see Jim."
"That's alright," Ben said.
And off they went to find the girls. They were in the quite lounge having a coffee and a good natter!
"Is there any coffee going, Jane? All this talking making me thirsty."
"Make that two, please."
"What have you two been up to then? You have been gone for quite a while!"
"Well, I'm afraid we have some disturbing news for you about our friend Joshua."
"Oh," they both said together. "This sounds serious."
"Well, it may not be as bad!"
"Go on, tell all."
"That conversation I had with Jim early brought to light why Joshua is on that island."
"We're all ears" said Jane. "The interesting part is that they think he may have something to do with smuggling."
"Oh, you have got to be joking!"
"We thought you would say that, Jane, but until they speak to him we don't know."
"So what you're saying is he might have to come back to the main land after all."
"There is not much more we can do, this coffee tastes good. Any more in the pot?"
"No, I'll go and make us all a fresh pot, it's been a very hot day. Do you fancy a sandwich, anybody?"
"Oh, that would be lovely, Jane, thanks."
"Back in a mo!"
"She's a darling, I think she is a bit cut up about Josh."
"Well, she might get a chance to see him again, I know she wants too. I think we will be docking soon in Santa Pola, so tomorrow, everyone, we had better be getting all our things together."
"Jane, those sandwiches look lovely and the coffee smells good. We shall be sorry to leave this ship."
"There is always next year."
"Oh, no, here she goes again! Another adventure not likely, not for me any way," said Ben. "This has put me off for life!"
"I for one think it has been quite exciting, I never dreamt I would be stranded on a remote island."
"None of us did, Jane. I don't think we ever want to again.
"Well, anyway we all survived and we have learnt from our experience. Haven't we?"
"Yes, put it like that I suppose we have" said Bill. "I am going to get ready for dinner, anybody else coming?"
"Yes, we won't be long."
An hour later they were sitting at the table, of course they forgot it was their last night on board the Princess Marigold. The captain made a touching fair well speech for them, all he said it was the most enjoyable voyage he had ever done; of course the castaways knew who he was referring to, and they all smiled at each other, they were happy now they were going home.

Afterwards they went down to the quiet lounge so they could chat to Jim and to thank him for everything he had done for them.
"It's been my pleasure, I have met the loveliest people, we will have to keep in touch with each other."
"Yes, that would be nice, and perhaps we can book a another voyage with your ship next year."
"You can count me out on that one" said Ben.
Jane laughed and said: "I knew that was coming. Ben hasn't really liked this journey one little bit."
"No, I haven't said Ben I never want to see water, fish or bad weather again."
"Oh, Ben, shut up and drink your coffee; it's getting cold. At least we are safe, that's all that matters, isn't it, Jim?"
"Yes, Jane, it is thank goodness we picked you up; you could have been there for a very long time."
"Yes, we were lucky and we are very grateful, Jim."
"Oh, I think it's time to talk to your parents. I'll just see if number one put you trough, be back in a mo! Yes, he's talking to them now. I think it's best if one of you go."
"I'll go up," said Bill, "and I will tell them all the news and I will tell you, chaps, what they say. Is that OK everyone!"
"Yes, that's fine by us."
"Off you go, don't keep them waiting otherwise you will block the shipping channel."
"Right see you later."
"Well I'm going down to finish the packing, are you coming, Jane?"
"Yes, bye for now."
"Jane has certainly enjoyed this trip it's done her good to get away for a while. We didn't realize we would be away this long though!"
"Still you will be home soon."
"Yes, then we can get back to normal. I have still quite a lot of work to do in the house, we only moved in a few months ago. This was supposed to be our retiring home, hoping for peace and quiet, and look what happens. Jane decided to have an adventure, nearly got us killed... but never mind, it certainly was an experience, but I wouldn't like to go through it again."
"Oh, here comes Bill, looking rather pleased with himself. Had a good natter then, Bill? How are they all?"
"They all fine, they send their love, they can't wait to see you all again. I told them we are getting a car to take us back, and that our boat is being brought back on dry land again."
"That's alright then everyone's happy again."
"Well, I'm of to my bed coming Ben?"
"Yes, I am. Goodnight all."
"Night, Ben, sleep well."

Almost home at last

Four days later they had arrived in Cartagena, the weather had change considerably, there was a lot of noise from the other ships and small vessels, it looked a pretty sight. Jane took out her camera: it was such a wonderful moment! They were home at last; it took quite a while to get into the dock lanes as they had to wait for clearance. Soon the ship's hooter could be heard and they were ready for their turn. Slowly she made her way into the harbour, and sure enough, guess who was waiting for them! Yes, of course, Bouncer was there barking and pulling on his lean.

"There, I told you he wouldn't have forgotten us; let's get down the gangplank and say hello."

Everyone was talking and laughing at the same time, so John had to shout to make himself heard.

"Hello, there shipmates, glad you survived the journey, did you have a good crossing?"

"Not bad" said Ben.

"A bit rough at times though," said Bill, "but we're OK now we're back on dry land again; we all can't wait to get home."

"Yes, that's right" said the girls together.

"Well, then what are we waiting for? Let's go home."

It wasn't long before they were at their house. Jean couldn't hold her excitement any longer, she cried out to Jane: "What a wonderful place you have here! Oh, look at the squirrels! Aren't they cute? And the parakeets, what lovely colours they have!"

Jane and Ben laughed: "This is nothing, wait till we take you to the park."

"Oh, but first we must have something to eat, I'm starving," said Ben. "I think we all are."

"Wait a moment, I think Shirley has a meal ready for us all, let's go and see then we can show off our house too."

"Oh, John, that's very kind of you, but you shouldn't have gone to so much trouble."

"Well, Shirley insisted that we should, we knew you would be hungry after your long journey so let's go and enjoy it."

With that they all went inside and what a welcome!

"You old dark horse! John, you kept this quiet, didn't you?"

"Yes, we thought it was best."

"Oh, look, Jane, isn't he cute? How old is he?"

"Actually, Ben, it's a she; we are thinking of breeding from her."

"And what does Bouncer think of her?"

"Oh, he adores her and they haven't been apart since."

"Oh, dear, that's going to be a bit difficult now."

"Well, not really, the way we see it we still could take them to the park."

"Yes, I suppose we could."

"Well, are you going to sit there all day or are you coming to eat? It's getting cold and I do hate serving cold meals."

“OK, were coming now.”
And boy, what a lovely meal it was! And everyone was trying to talk at the same time, the dogs also tried to join in, but John firmly told them to go and lie down in the basket, which they did.
“Oh, look at that,” said Jane. “How sweet they look, must take a photo.”
Shirley felt happy now her friends were back home safe at last. She longed to her more about Josh but thought it could wait another day: they all looked so exhausted; they had one more drink then they went their separate ways. Ollie tried to chase after Bouncer, but John called her back: “We’ll go to the park tomorrow.” She did a little *woof* and then she went to lie down.
The next morning they woke up late; when Ben came downstairs the phone was ringing, it sounded urgent.
“Hello,” said Ben. “Who’s calling?”
“Hello there, shipmate, it’s Jim from the ship. I’ve some news about Josh.”
“Go on,” said Ben. “I am all ears.”
“The police have been in contact with me about him, they want you all to go down to the police station to talk to the cid in charge. Can you do that? At your convenience, of course.”
“OK, thanks, Jim. I’ll see what the girls say, bye for now.”
When they were all together Ben told them what Jim had said. Jane still was convinced that he couldn’t be involved in any wrong doing, he just wasn’t that sort.
“There, I told you he was up to no good and now I am sure of knowing what they say.”
“You shouldn’t judge a book by its cover.”
With that Jean laughed: “No, Jane’s right, I believe in what she says. I liked him too, I think he should be left alone.”
Ben went to get his pipe, and taking his coffee with him went out into the patio, after all he had some serious thinking to do.
“Come on, Bouncer, let’s play ball.”
“Woof” said Bouncer; that was his favourite game. He was happy now his master was back in control.

Getting to the bottom of Joshua

The next morning they went down to the local police station, they were lead into a small back room where they wouldn’t be disturbed. The sargent offered them tea or coffee, he soon put them at ease, he was easy to talk to. Jane told him how they came to be on the island and that Josh helped them to survive by showing them how to catch fish and wildlife. Jane could sense Ben’s disapproval, but didn’t take any notice of it.
“You have been helpful. We would like to talk to the boys now, help yourself to some more coffee.”
“Thank you, we will. See you later, dear” said Jane.

"OK."
"Shall we go and have a look round the shops?"
"Yes, why not? We can leave a message at the desks for the boys, it looks as though they will be here for some time."
"Yes, I think they will, why? I don't know what all the fuss about is.
"You still think Josh is not involved, don't you, Jane?"
"Yes, I do, and no one can change my mind."
"Oh, well," said Jean. "We will have to wait and see."
They went in search of the shops, not far from the station; for a change the weather was quite warm, in any case it was better than it had been for ages. It felt good to feel the warmth of the sun again and it was lovely to be back on home ground. The girls were enjoying themselves so much that they had forgotten the boys and the time.
"Goodness me," said Jane. "Come on, it's time we headed back to the boys."
"Oh, there you are, we were just coming to look for you, have you had coffee?"
"Yes" said Jane.
"And a bun" said Jean.
"Well, we are thirsty, so where is this café you went to?"
"Oh, it's not far! Come on, we will show you."
Soon they were all talking at once, until Bill told them to calm down and let Ben get a word in, otherwise they would be here all night.
"What did the police say about Josh then?" said Jane. "Are they going to look for him?"
"They have asked us to go with them back to the island, also so we can show them where our boat is; it has to be bought back to the harbour."
"Well, what do we do about Bouncer? We can't ask John to have him again."
"No, we have thought about that, so I suggested that I stay behind and you others go, after all I really don't want to see him again."
"OK, that's alright by us; we will go. I'll give the officer in charge a call on the mobile and find out when he wants to go."
"When are you thinking of going home, Bill and Jane?"
"Well, we can't go until this has been sorted out, then we will make plans."
When they got home Jane went to phone mum and dad, she was getting quite excited about seeing Josh again, and she couldn't wait to tell mum all about it. She dialled the number and mum answered it.
"Goodness me!" she cried. "You sound very excited, dear; what's the matter?"
"Well, mum, guess what! We are going back to the island next week to pick up Josh," Jane said. "I would see him again, but I didn't think I would be seeing him so soon."
"Oh, now I can see why you are so excited; are you all going then dear?"
"No, someone has to stay behind to look after Bouncer, and that's Ben. Oh, also John has bought himself a puppy just like Bouncer and he his going to breed from her, and Jean might be getting one too."
"When is she coming home then?"
"Well as soon as this mess has all been sorted out, mum."
"I've missed her so much these past few months, and you of course. When are you coming home?"

"Well, we were thinking of Christmas, which is not too far away."
"That's something to look forward too then, have a good trip over to the island and phone me as soon as you get back." With that she was gone.
Jane was a bit worried about her mum, she didn't sound like her old cheerful self and she went off to find Ben. She found him smoking his pipe on the patio; Bouncer was playing with his ball having a great time and chasing the squirrels.
"There you are" said Jane.
"Oh, hello, dear, just having a quiet smoke. How was mum?"
"Well, she sounded as though she was keeping something back from me, she didn't like the idea of me going back to the island."
"Well, I am not over the moon about it myself, but you won't be gone long this time, and as you are going in a helicopter it will be quite different than last time."
"Yes, you're right about that. I just hope that they are barking up the wrong tree, that's all."
Jean came and told them that dinner was ready. Bouncer came running in.
"Steady on, Bouncer, you nearly knocked the tea over."
He rushed to his bowl and he had a bite from it. *Good, this is my favourite*, and within seconds it was gone.
"Goodness me," said Jane. "You were hungry."
Bouncer went to lie down in his basket and went to sleep. As soon as they all sat down to dinner the phone rang.
"I'll go and answer it," said Jane. "That was the police again, they are thinking of going out next week; can we be ready by then?"
"I think so," said Bill. "How long do you think we shall be away for this time?"
"Well, as long as Joshua cooperates shouldn't take long, let's say about two days at the most."
"That's good," said Ben. "Then we can put all this behind us and start enjoying ourselves again."
Jane didn't say a word but went in search of a good book to read, she was glad that most of the housework was done thanks to Jean helping her; she was going to miss her when she went back to England.
Ben came out with Bouncer, just taking him for his evening walk: "Do you want to come along?"
"No thanks dear, I'd rather finish my book."
"Everything alright, love? You're very quiet."
"Yes, I am OK, thanks, just thinking about mum, that's all."
"Well, if you're sure I'll be on my way, see later."
"Bye then, dear"
Away he went humming to himself. He took Bouncer to the park, he knew he loved that place. He let him off his lead away from the duck pond, Bouncer went into the woods near by while Ben sat on the bench near the pond, he was really worried about Jane, she was really taken this too far. *When she comes back I thing I will talk to Jean, and see if she can go back with her for a while; she could see mum at the same time*. He was about to call Bouncer, but there was no need, he came and sat down beside him.

"Hello there, have you enjoyed your run? Goodness me! What have you got there? Drop it, there's a good boy."
When he dropped it Ben felt sad for the poor thing, it was a duck that had wondered too far from the pond. Ben picked it up and took it to the gamekeeper; he gave Bouncer a right telling off.
"Sorry about that," said Ben. "He does chase ducks, but he never usually catches them; all he wants to do is play with them."
"I don't thing that pastime should be encouraged, one day Bouncer could be hurt. He's such a lovely dog and that would be a shame."
"Well, we had better make for home, otherwise we will have the girls telling us off next."
When Ben arrived home he went into the kitchen. Boy, it did smell good, he hadn't realized how hungry he was till now.
"Hello there, Ben," said Bill. "Had a good walk?"
"Yes we did, didn't we Bouncer?"
"What's he been up to?"
"Oh, he's only gone and caught a duck from the pond; it went wondering of on it's own and Bouncer found it, but this time he decided to bring it back to me."
"Oh dear, we thought you had been gone a long time, what did the gamekeeper say?"
"Well, he told Bouncer off, and he came back to me with his tail between his legs, it looked quite funny really."
"I bet it did," said Jane. "No wonder he has gone straight for his basket, he always does when he's been told off; anyway dinners ready, and yours, Bouncer, so you can stop looking sorry for yourself now."
"Woof, woof!" he said and made for his bowl.
All the talk around the dinner table was about Joshua much to his annoyance. Much to the girls surprise the boys offered to wash up and make the tea; the two girls went into the lounge and Bouncer decided to follow them.
"Hello, fellow," said Jane. "You have been a naughty dog today, don't forget: no more catching ducks." As if he understood every word Jane was saying, he put a paw on her lap he looked at Jane, who couldn't help but smile at him. "Now look at him," said Jane. "It looks like butter wouldn't melt in his mouth."
"Yes, I know. I shall miss him when we go home, which won't be to far away now, as soon as we get back from the island. Do you think he will come back with us this time?"
"I'm afraid he hasn't much choice this time." said Jane, "they are convinced he is their man, but I hope not other wise Ben will be saying *I told you so*!"
"It makes a change for the boys to do the washing up, don't you think?" said Jean.
"Yes I was surprised they did."
"I wonder what their up to."
"We will have to wait and see" said Jane.
"I'm going to have a hot shower, then I am having an early night" said Jean.
"I've got to finish this book, it seems to be taken ages."
"Sleep well then," said Jean, "see you in the morning."
"I'll stay up a bit longer, I want to speak to Ben about Josh."
"OK then best of luck."

Ben came into the room and said to Jane: "All finished now, tidy as a new pin."
"Thanks, dear, that was kind of you, well that's the least we could do after a good meal like that; you really are a good cook."
"Well, thank you dear, now tell me what you are really up to, I know you too well; there must be something afoot."
With a smile on his face, he said: "Well, maybe there is, but only if you agree."
"Well, I'm listening."
"I know you're worried about mum, so when you come back from the island…"
"Yes," said Jane "go on!"
"Well, why don't you go back to England with Jean and have a quiet holiday?
"That's a good idea, I might just do that, but don't book the flight just yet, not until I get back.
Oh there was some thing else on my mind, Ben, it's about Josh. When I see him again I was thinking of inviting him to our home, what do you think of that?"
"Oh, no, why here? Won't he be staying at the police station?"
"Well, possibly if they do find that he has been involved, but other than that he won't have any where to stay."
"Well, we could but him up in a hotel somewhere."
"Is that a no, then?"
"Let's see what the outcome of the trip over to the island turns out."
"You know, Ben, there isn't anything going on between him and me, you know."
"It doesn't look like that from where I am sitting."
"Ben, how could you ever think that of me! You're my only true love, after all these years you should know that by now."
"I do, love, but every time you talk about him you can see it in your eyes."
"But I don't hardly know the man, I just feel sorry for him, that's all it is," with that Jane went to kiss Ben. "Please, don't let us fall out over him."
"All right, dear, enough talk about him."
"Are you coming up?"
"Yes, I'll just let Bouncer out, won't be long."

No one on the island

The following Tuesday the helicopter came for them, the weather was quite calm, just a few clouds, but nothing to worry about. The girls were very excited in seeing Josh again, little did they no what unforeseen things lied ahead of them. It wasn't long before they reached the island; it still looked the same old island. They touched down very quietly, Bill and the pilot and the officer had to run to catch up with them.
"Steady on, you two, you will see him soon enough."
They went towards the cave, cold and deserted, and then they started to call him, but to no avail: he just wasn't around.

Flabbergasted, but not too surprised, they turned to Bill and the others.
"Well, my dears," the officer said. "It looks as though we were right; sorry girls now we have cause for alarm, but don't worry, we will catch him sooner or later."
"Maybe so," said Jane, "but hang on! Where has our boat gone? We left it somewhere near here, I'm sure we did, didn't we Bill?
Bill had been quiet all this time, he could not quite take in what he was seeing, everywhere on the island looked deserted and lonely even the animals were quiet.
At last Bill found his voice: "Yes, Jane you're right, we did leave the boat somewhere near here. But I think it was further up river. If you remember we started off aright, then we had that slight accident with the boat, and that's where the ship picked us up."
"Yes, that's right" said Jane.
"Of course it was. Come on, let's see if it's still there, I bet it isn't."
They ran back to the helicopter and went in search of their boat.
It wasn't long before they came to the area, but as they already knew the boat wasn't there.
"Well, I'll be blown, I still think he is innocent though" said Jane, was so looking forward in seeing him again.
"Well, I'll better radio in and find out what we have to do next."
"Can we go back tonight?" Bill asked the pilot.
"OF course we can, no problem," and soon they were on their way home.

More about Joshua

When they arrived home Ben was quite surprised to see them.
"Hello there, I didn't expect you back this early, anything wrong? Are you girls alright? Will some one tell me what's going on?"
"Let's have a cup of tea first," said Jane. "I think we all need one. What about you two? You can have something stronger if you like."
"Yes, please, we would like a cool beer if you have any."
"Yes, of course," said Ben, "then you can tell me everything; it all seems very mysterious, I must say."
They all sat around the fire and told Ben everything, about how Josh wasn't on the island and the poor animals looked sorry for themselves, it was a very cold and empty place to be in.
Ben said after a while: "Well, what about the boat? What are we going to do about that?"
"Well," said Bill, "we will have to inform the harbour and tell them it is missing, then we shall have to sort out the insurance for it. Goodness me, some adventure this has turned out to be."
"We shall have to be on our way," said the officer, "we shall have to look into this further, it might have to go to Interpol and do a world wide search for him; if he wasn't in trouble before he certainly is now, you mark my word."

Jane didn't say anything, she was to upset about the whole affair.
"Well, we will be off now then, thank you for the drinks."
"Right," said Ben, "we'll be in touch then, see you soon."
As soon as they were gone, Jean said: "How about us going out for a meal tonight, and lighten ourselves up? What do you say, Jane?"
"That's a good idea."
So off they all went to get ready. It wasn't long before they were enjoying their meal, it was one of the best restaurants in town, it always had a good reputation and the food was good too.
"Right," said Ben to Bill when the girls went to the lady's, "was it really that bad on the island?"
"Yes, it was," said Bill. "The girls didn't want to stay on it too long. Jane was upset about Josh not being there and now she is worried for his safety too."
"Oh, dear," said Ben. "It's all a mess, isn't it?"
"The police still have 5 in custody though they are going to talk to them again about Josh and see if they can shed some light into his disappearance. You never know what they will come up with."
Just then the girls came back Jane overheard the last remark: "Now who are we talking about?"
"The police are going to question the men they have got in custody."
"Yes, that does make sense," said Jane, "let's hope they find him soon, now let's be away home; it's been a very tiring day."
Ben open the door and Bouncer came running towards him: "Hello, old fellow, what have you been up to? Oh, no, Bouncer, you bad dog, you have chewed my pipe and I haven't a spare one, now I shall have to get a new one tomorrow. No, I am not going to make a fuss of you, I thought you had got over this stage. In your basket, I am not making a fuss of you tonight."
Jane and Jean came in, they couldn't help but laugh at Bouncer.
"Don't laugh at him," said Ben, "look what he's done to my pipe."
"Oh, dear," said Jane. "Never mind, you can get a new one, it's not the end of the world."
"I know, love, but I've had this pipe for ages and it's not the same when you have to blend in with a new one. Ask any piper and they'll tell you the same, still you ladies don't understand,
do they Bill?"
"I'm saying nothing, I'm not a smoker, end of story, mate."
With that Bill and Jane went up stairs to bed; it had certainly been a tiring but fun day, they never knew they would ever go up in a helicopter. Soon the household was very quite apart from Bouncer snoring downstairs. They all slept in rather late, much to their surprise it had gone 11 when they all came down.
"What's everyone having for breakfast?" said Jane yawning.
"It looks like you want to go back to bed, never mind breakfast, Jane. Did you have a bad night? You were tossing and turning a bit."
"Sorry if I disturbed you," said Jane. "It's this thing about Josh. I can't get over it, why would he want to disappear like that? That's what I would like to know."

"Yes, we all would, but never mind that now, come and have something to eat and some coffee; it will wake you up."
"Alright, maybe I will, thank you Ben," she went to kiss him on his forehead. "Are you going to get a new pipe today? You look lost without one."
"Yes, I think I will. What are you all doing today?"
"Well," said Bill, "I would like to go into town to get some last minute things before we go home."
"Jane wanted to as well."
"In that case why don't we all go? We can have a snack there as well, I don't think Jane will be up to cooking today, she's rather tired I'll give her the day off."
"What do you think Jane?"
"Yes, that's very sweet of you," she gave him a kiss too, "goodness I am being fuss over today."
They had a lovely day, no one mentioned Josh, the island or anything, which made a refreshing change. They were discussing Jean and Bill going back home and Jane going with them, at first she wasn't sure if she could leave Ben on his own, but then this time he had Bouncer and John and Shirley next door so he wasn't really on his own. Jane was going home in a few weeks, she wanted to stay to see the outcome of Josh.
A few weeks later they received a phone call from the police who was taking care of Joshua's case.
"Can we come and see you tomorrow? We think we have found The Mermaid, but we would like you to identify it."
"Certainly you can," said Ben. "Anytime in the day would be OK."
"Looking forward to meet you then."
Ben went into the kitchen, Bill was having a late lunch; he could tell by his face that it was good news: "Well," he said, "what did the police say? And have they found Josh?"
"Is there any tea in the pot? I could certainly do with one."
"Well," said Bill, are you going to tell us?"
"All in good time" said Ben.
Finally he broke his silence: "Well, would you believe it?"
"Well, I never. What are we going to do? We shall have to stay over somewhere?"
"Yes, we will. Jane's not back from shopping yet then?"
"No, she rang and said she was having a snack somewhere in town with Jean and going to book her holiday."
"That will cheer her up then. I know she's missing her mum."
"Do you think it's The Mermaid then, Ben?"
"Yes, it sounds very much like it."
"So when are we going?"
"The officer is coming to see us tomorrow morning; he has some photos of it."
"I can't wait to see it again, it was a lovely boat to sail."
"Yes, I agree there it was."
"I wonder where Josh is now."

"Oh, him! He could be anywhere. I think Bouncer's getting ready for his walk, look at this, Bill, he brings us his lead now."
"Yes," said Bill. "I shall miss him when we go home, maybe one day we will get a dog like him, properly one of John's pups, who knows?"
"Oh, hello you two, enjoyed your lunch?"
"Yes, thanks, are you just going or coming?"
"Oh, just going love," Ben said, "won't be long."
"Bill can fill you in about the phone call we had earlier."
"Oh, that sounds intriguing, let's hear more."
After Ben had gone, Bill told her all about The Mermaid.
"At least they think it's it."
"So where on earth is Josh?" asked Jane.
"That they don't know yet, the other men didn't know much about him either so you could say they drew a blank, but they are still keen to find him, so at least he could clear his name."
"You don't suppose something horrible has happen to him?" said Jane, alarm bells were ringing in her ears.
"No, I don't think he would take that way out, but you never know, anyway did you book the flight? And when are we going?"
"Well, Jane wanted to stay until this business of Josh is cleared up, but it looks as though it could go on for sometime."
By the time Ben came back it was quite dark.
"Any one for a nightcap?" said Jane.
"Oh, I'll have a brandy, do you want one, Bill?"
"Yes, please, that will be lovely. What are you having, Jean?"
"Have we any sherry left?"
"Yes, a bit," said Jane. "Must get some more tomorrow."
Bouncer was in his basket fast asleep.
"That walk tired him out," said Jane, "he looks like butter won't melt in his mouth."
"Yes, he's settling down now, at least he didn't go chasing the ducks again. Having a dog certainly keeps one fit."
"It seems to have done you good," said Bill. "I think we shall have one when we get home."
"Well, everyone, I'm off to bed. Have a good night;" said Ben, "that dog has tired me out tonight."
"OK, dear, be up soon."
"Night," said Jean. "Sleep well."
The following morning the police officer came to see them.
"Oh, I'm glad you are all here. Can we go on Thursday to check the boat out? Where the boat was found the police are getting in the divers to check that he has not drowned."
He could see the alarm in Jane's face and Jean put her arms around to comfort her.
"Well, I'll be off now then, see you on Thursday, Ben, and you, Bill."
"OK," they both said together, "see you soon."

The girls were in the lounge having a stiff drink; they didn't usually drink during the day, but on this sad occasion they felt they needed it. The days went by so quickly, soon it was Thursday. Bill and Ben went with the officer to see if it was their boat, Bill was praying it was, so they could get it back to the rightful owner and then it would be out of their hands.
"Bye then, we will give you a call when we get there, wish us luck."
"Oh, you're off then," said Jane. "Take care and don't forget to phone us."
"No, dear we won't." With that they were gone.
The girls busied themselves all day, only stopping for a snack, as they were all going out for a meal later. Outside the wind was getting up and it looked like rain.
"I'm glad we went out yesterday, Jane, aren't you?"
"Yes I am; it looks like were in for a good old down pour. We haven't had much rain here lately; it will do the flowers good."
"I wonder how the boys are getting on."
"Yes, I wonder; they should be ringing us soon."
Just at that precise moment the phone rang!
"Hello, is that Ben? We were just talking about you; well, is it the boat? And did you find Josh?"
"One question at a time, love. Yes, it is The Mermaid. It's not to badly damaged, just a little lick of paint will soon put it right."
"Oh, that's good then. Any news of Josh?"
"Afraid not, dear, but the police think he may have drowned after all, they're looking for him now; it will be a while before they can tell us anything, so it looks as if we might be staying over night. Will you girls be OK on your own?"
"Yes, of course we will. We have Bouncer and each other, just find Josh alive, Ben, that's all I ask."
"We'll do our best," said Bill and Ben, "see you girls later."
"Yes, bye for now."
When Jane had finished her conversation, she dialled mum's phone number.
"Hello," said mum, "oh, it's you, Jane. How's everything in sunny Spain then?"
"Not so sunny now though, mum, it's pouring of rain."
"Did they find the boat then?" said mum. "I've been so worried that you might have to pay out a lot of money for the insurance."
"No, don't worry about that: yes they have found it, and all it needs is a lick of paint and it will be as good as new, so Ben says, but there's no sign of Josh, we fear the worse, he was a lonely old man mum, but a good man."
"He certainly took care of you on that island, didn't he?"
"Yes, he did, he saved us from starvation anyway. Oh, how is dad now? Has he got over his cancer?"
"Well, actually no. I'm afraid, Jane, it's come back again. They are treating him but this time it's got hold of him, that's why I wanted you to come home. It would cheer him up no end, love. So when are you coming? So I can get things ready for you. We can't wait to see you all again, it's been a long time."

"We should be home in two weeks, mum, it's not to far away now, we will let you know the flight details later. Bye for now, love to you both, see you soon."
The next few days were rather hectic for the Johnson's household, first they had to bring The Mermaid back into dry docks again. Ben and Bill took it upon themselves to do the painting, gradually it was looking as good as new. It was really a wonderful boat and they were going to miss it terribly.
On the way home Ben said to Bill: "You know, wouldn't it be nice if we could buy her?"
"Dream on, mate," Bill said. "You're not serious."
"Well, why not? It would be great if we could."
"Yes, but I bet the insurance would be high."
"I don't know," said Ben. "It's worth looking into, when I get home I shall talk to Jane about it."
"OK," Bill said, "if she agrees count me in. I am very fond of the old girl myself."
"Alright, I'll let you know. By the way, when are you going home? Did Jane say?"
"Yes, I think it's next Thursday, Ben."
"Oh, that's OK then, Jane's looking forward in seeing her mum again, although she did say some thing about dad's cancer returning which doesn't sound very good."
"Oh dear! That's a shame, Ben, he is such a lovely man, isn't he?"
"Yes, he is. We will know more when Jane goes home."
Soon they arrived home and Jane and Jean ware waiting for them.
"Hello, what is going on here? They don't wait at the gate normally, something's happened, I am sure. Come on, let's go and see."
"Oh, Ben and Bill, were so glad your home!"
"Why, love, what ever is the matter? You both look as though you have seen a ghost."
"Come in both of you and we will tell you all about it."
Jane went to make some tea, Jean started to tell them about Josh.
"Oh, my goodness, another fine mess. He hadn't any family you know, so who is going to sort out is funeral?
"The poor man, no wonder Jane is worried about it. Where have they taken his body, Jean?"
"Oh, he is in Santa Pola, the police want us to go and identify him."
"What, all of us?"
"Yes," said Jane, "all of us."
"Well, I think this calls for some stronger then tea. Anyone else's going to join me?
"Yes, please we all will, thank you."
"When are we going then?" Ben asked.
"Oh, on Friday they are bringing a car round for us at around ten a.m. He can't be put to rest till after the post mortem."
"Who is going to bury him then?"
"Well, I think it will have to be us."
"Oh no, you are joking?" Jane's white face said it all.
"Where are we going to get the money from? Have you thought about that?"
"Well, yes, the police say he can have a paws funeral."
"Well, I'll be blown, you have thought of every thing, have not you?"

"Well, yes, I have. Ben, remember Josh didn't have any of his family left so someone's got to bury him."
"Well, but it that way I suppose you're right. We have a few days yet before Friday, so let's try and not worry till then."
He went off to find his new pipe; it wasn't so good as his old one. He went out into the garden with Bouncer at his heels.
"It's a lovely evening, Bouncer summer is almost here. Poor old Josh, fancy dying like that, all on his own, it makes you go cold even to think about it."
"Oh, there you are, Ben. I am so sorry to have had to tell you the news, I know what you thought of him but I would like to just do this one thing for him, you do understand, don't you, Ben?"
He put his arm around her, and said: "Yes, my dear, believe me I do, so don't worry. I will be with you every step of the way, so stop being sad but remember him as we all knew him, OK?"
"Yes, you're right, darling, I will" she kissed him and quietly went back indoors. Jane and Bill had already gone to bed and all was quit once more, what a day it had turned out to be! The following day the girls went into town to do some last minute shopping before going home, it was late spring and the weather was getting warmer, both here and in England. A few weeks later they were on their way home. When they arrived in Scotland mum was at the gate waiting for them.
"Hello, I am glad you arrived safely, did you have a good trip?"
"Yes, thanks, mum, it was a bit choppy but only for a short while."
"Oh, that's good then. Come away in, I have dinner ready for you."
"We thought you would have, bless you," Jane gave her a big hug. "I have missed you, mum," said Jane, "we all have."
"Never mind, you're all home now."
They went into the dining room, the table was set already, mum certainly went to town, it was a lovely meal. They were all talking at once, mum had to tell them to slow down, it was making her head spin.
"Well, now," Bill said. "What is this we have been hearing about dad? Anyway, where is he? With all you talking at once I never got a word in edge way."
"I'm afraid dad is in hospital having some test done about his cancer. Yes, I am afraid it's come back again and it's more serious this time."
"Oh, mum why didn't you tell us over the phone? You never tell us anything, you are naughty, but now we're here we will go and see him tomorrow."
"Well, I was going anyway; he will be pleased to see you all, we can get him something tomorrow. He is not eating much. The test are making him feel sick, still we can see when we get there."
When mum had gone to bed Jane said: "You know, this doesn't sound good, does it? Not the home coming we would have liked."
"No," said Bill. "It isn't poor old dad; he is such a nice man. I bet you he told mum not to tell us, you know what he is like."
"You can say that again," said Jane. "He always kept things from us. Still let's pray things are not as bad as they seem."

Tomorrow's another day

In the morning they heard mum busy in the kitchen.
"Oh, mum, why let us do the breakfast? Give yourself a rest."
"Thanks, Jane, but I would rather keep busy; it stops me from worrying."
"Yes I know," said Jane. "But you look awful."
"I am worried sick about dad. I think he will not get over this cancer scare this time."
"No, I am afraid that's what we all think; anyway let's sees how he is when we go and visit him. Now how about that breakfast?"
"Oh, here comes Bill and Jean. Hello you two, are you hungry?"
"I could eat a horse" said Bill.
"Me too" said Jane.
"Well, come on then, let's eat, and you can fill me in on all the latest news. I need cheering up."
"Well," said Bill, "you know about our trip. Gosh what a trip that was! Ben didn't like it at all, he said no more adventures for him."
Mum laughed: "No, he wasn't the adventurous type. Jane is though."
"Yes, didn't we know it? She had us doing all sorts of things on the island, poor old Josh didn't know what to make of her."
"What about the funeral then? Who will do it if he has no family to speak of?"
"The police will pay for some of it and we'll do the rest. He his going to be buried in a little church in Santa Pola. The police arranged that before we came out, soon it will be all over and then we can get our lives back to normal. Now mum what are your plans for the future?"
"Well, dear, I have thought about it, what I shall do is keep the house on here and let it out for rent and then I will come and live in that granny flat you mention. Will that be OK?"
"Oh, mum," said Jane. "Of course it will; let's see how dad is today, it might not be as bad as it seems."
When they arrived at the hospital the nurse was waiting for them.
"Mrs. Jones I am afraid we have had to put your husband in one of our side wards, it got a bit noisy in the main ward. We thought it was best as he needs to be kept quiet, however he isn't in any pain, we have given him some pain relief. You may find him a bit sleepy; if you need me just press the buzzer. Here we are then, he has spotted you already, that's a good sign."
"Hello, love, oh, it's good to see you. I've missed you so much."
"Me too," said Joyce. "Look who I've bought to see you today."
"Hello, love, how are you all? And there's Bill and Jean! When did you get in?"
"Hello, dad, good to see you. We arrived on Monday, you have given us quite a scare, you know."

"Sorry about that, love, but these things happen to pop up with out you realising it. The nurses are taking good care of me though, they put me in here so I can get some rest. I start my, chemo tomorrow it should give me more time.
"Oh, love, I am glad to hear it! I have been so worried I might lose you."
"Don't worry, love, I am not going anywhere just yet, the doctors and nurses will see to that. Now let's talk about Spain. How is Bouncer? What has he been up to lately?"
"He is still chasing ducks, he has learnt one or two new tricks, and Jean is thinking about getting one; it will give Bill some exercise. Are we tiring you, dad?" said Jane?
"No, love, it's these horrible tablets I am taking; they make me thirsty and sleepy."
"Well, at least it kills the pain love."
"Yes, it does, but I wish the cancer hadn't come back."
"We will just have to make what time we have left together a good one. Jane's here for a while and we will come in again on Tuesday. You have a good rest now and we will see you soon."
"OK, dear, bye for now, love, love you all."
Mum took them down town for a coffee and a snack, they were all very quite thinking of dad and of course Jane was thinking of Josh, she knew she shouldn't be but she was very fond of him and she felt saddened that he lived a very lonely life, and then having to die on his own too.
"What do you make of dad then, Jane," mum said suddenly, making them all jump.
"He is very poorly, that is obvious. We shall just have to take each day as it comes; don't look so worried mum we are here to support you every inch of the way. I am sure dad won't want you to be unhappy, he still could come home."
"I hope he will," said mum. "I hope he will."
She went off to pay the bill, and then they all made for home. It would soon be tea time, mum made some lovely sconces, they were the girls favourite, just as they sat down for tea the phone rang. Jane went to answer it: "Hello, love," said Jane, "anything wrong?"
"No, dear, just phoning to see how dad is. Did you get to see him today?"
"Yes, we did," said Jane. "I am afraid he his not too clever, he his on strong painkillers and starting his chemo tomorrow, we're told to come back on Thursday."
"So it is the big C, then" said Ben.
"Yes, I am afraid it is."
"Oh, dear and they are releasing Josh tomorrow."
"Well, I would like to stay and give mum some support, we can't leave her on her own; she is too worried about dad at the moment."
"I understand, love, I will go and see the officer tomorrow and see if we can do it at a later date."
"That would be a good idea."
"Give my love to him and mum."

"Of course, dear, I will, talk to you soon, bye for now."
"Was that Ben, dear?"
"Yes, mum, it was he; sends you both his love."
"That's was kind of him, he is such a nice man."
"I think so too."
Jane went into the kitchen to start on the washing up, but found jean had beaten her to it.
"Mum's having a rest in the conservatory, it's a lovely afternoon, the sun is shining through the window."
"Yes, all this worry isn't doing her any good either. We shall have to keep an eye on her."
At the weekend they went to see dad.
He still looked rather poorly, the doctors and nurses had taken very good care of him, while they were visiting him dad ask to be taken home.
"Oh, love, you know I would love to have you home, but I think you ought to stay here a bit longer, to build yourself up, don't you agree, Bill?"
"Yes, dad, she is right, we will still come and see you, of course, it's only your medication making you feel like this."
"Of course I know you're right, but it's so boring here, and I do miss you all."
"Yes, I know you do. I am sure it won't be long, love, and then you will be home."
They went back home feeling very sad, they knew he wouldn't come home. A few days they got the phone call they were dreading: dad had past away peacefully in his sleep. The sister said they could see him any time to say their goodbyes. There were a few tears, but as Bill said, he wouldn't want them to stay sad. A few days later they went to see him. Every one said how peaceful he looked, which made them feel a little better, now they had to arrange his funeral. At least he would get a proper one, not like poor old Josh.
The next few days they were very busy. Ben was coming over from Spain, and some of his dear friends were coming from all over the world, he was a very popular man. Mum had put her house in the hands of the letting agents in the town, Jean and Bill said goodbye to dad and mum and Jane; before Jean went she had some news of her own to tell them: yes, there was a baby on the way, it was due in the autumn.
"How long have you known?" said Jane.
"Oh, for a while now, but I wanted to make sure I was safe before I told any one, remember the last time, mum."
"I do, pet, and you were quite right to keep it so."
"Gosh," said Jane. "I am going to be an aunty at last; well done, Jean, I am proud of you."
"Me too" said mum. "Now let's drink to dad and the new baby. Oh, how wonderful!"
She went into the kitchen singing to herself.
"Now, that's cheered her up at least. We'll soon have her back with us again."
A few days later with Bill and Jean gone home; they were all preparing to go back to Spain this time taking mum with them, she was looking forward to her new life she

would have to manage without dad. When they arrived back in Spain the weather had turn rather warm, it was in the middle of summer and all the lovely flowers were out, even the almond trees were showing there wonderful colours. Mum loved her flat and they hardly knew she was there.
After a few weeks they put Joshua to rest too, in the end he had a lovely service, the police did him proud which made Jane very happy. Now they could all get on with their lives.

THE END

Este libro se terminó de imprimir en Madrid
en el mes de diciembre de 2010

edición **personal**
www.edicionpersonal.com